OK
A Novel

Kool A.D.

Published by Sorry House
Second edition 2016

ISBN 978-0-9888394-1-0
Book design by Adam Robinson
For distribution or wholesale information
visit sorry.house
@sorryhouse

4 MY FAM

1.

"Hello."

"Hello."

She was bad. Not bad as in bad but bad as in good. We were at the Missouri Lounge for some reason, over on San Pablo.

She had on a black bodysuit, red high heels, red lipstick. I was zooted off some high grade grass, a couple tequila shots and some Mexican beers, feeling brave.

"You look good."

She said something back but I honestly don't remember what it was, I was looking at the whole thing, the cat suit, the curvature, eye lashes, eye brows, red mouth, et cetera. Most impressive.

I opened up to her, told her I was a professional mugician by the name of KOOL MAN and she said she had heard of me. She told me she was a spiritualist by the name of Shirazi and I was like "Tight, tight." I felt like I had heard of her.

"I feel like I've heard of u."

"U have."

"Oh, O.K."

We carried on, talking, words and so forth, eye contact, a paw here or there, the whole nine. At the end of the night she slipped me her phone number and bit me on my arm, I was like "Damn."

We went off on our own waves, in and out of town, traveling, next time we linked up we got some coffee, drove around in her white Ferrari La Ferrari talking, smoking joints dipped in hash oil. Her family had done some international fleeing but made a decent buck in petroleum and other resources.

We ended up in a Spanish style house in Paradise Hills, a cutty little hood nestled twixt El Cerrito, Kensington and South Kensington.

We had some tea, smoked some hookah, smoked some hash. The record player played John Coltrane and then it played Alice Coltrane. We smashed.

We smoked a blunt on the balcony, it was a little cold out now.

"Now that we're married u have to convert to Islam.

"When did we get married?"

"We'll drive down to Orange County tonite I know a 24-hour mosque down there."

Sounded wavy.

"O.K."

We ate some vegan chocolate truffles and a couple adderalls a piece, climbed back in the 'rari and drove down. Foregoing the scenic route on the 1, we mainlined down the 5, fell into convoy with a gold '88 Caddy Deville in front and an 18 wheeler transporting Pink Cat products heading up the rear. We were all going a hunnit. The soundtrack was all 2Pac.

We made it to the mosque, paid our yaper.

The Imam was like, "Repeat after me: LA ILLAHA ILLALLAH, MUHAMMADUN RASULULLAH"

So I said: "LA ILLAHA ILLALLAH, MUHAMMADUN RASULULLAH"

Then I signed on the dotted line: MUHAMMAD X cuz that was my new name now.

She felt since I had changed my name it was only fair that she change hers too so she picked KHADIJA X.

I was a new mane, forged by Allah's solar heat, brimming with all types of Kundalinis and Kundalinettes, chakras blazing, zooming hard, jamming fierce, God in the building, Jah Rastafari 1 tru GOD en el nombre del Padre, el Hijo, el Espiritu Santo, 1 luv, Allah Hu Akbar.k

Most people, whether they want to believe it or not, don't actually believe in anything. They might think they believe in things but they don't, they walk around in a haze disguised as actual beliefs... the so-called beliefs disintegrate upon the slightest examination but the haze is thick and the so-called beliefs dart and dodge within that haze so as to never be caught in plain view. I used to live like this but my conversion to Islam burned away the fog and strengthened my hazy noncommittal half-beliefs into firm theological convictions.

Naw, just playing I still do my thing.

But on the real, when I said "LA ILLAHA ILLALLAH, MUHAMMADUN RASULULLAH" I did feel a burst of clarity and that clarity doesn't just evaporate, some of it lingers on the corners of the consciousness ready to pop off if need be.

My bride Khadija X kissed me on my newly Muslim lips.

"That was our second wedding, the third one is at my girl Medina's house."

Some spot out in Silverlake. We scraped on over there, she had a valet.

There was a dear's head on the wall.

The dear head was like, "bruh get me a shot of mescal, its up on the fridge."

I poured dude a shot and then I poured one for myself.

"Yal want some mescal?"

Medina said yes.

KHADIJA X, my bride, said no.

Poured a third shot.

Medina introduced us to the dear head.

"This is Changey."

"We met."

Shots all around; me, Changey, Medina.

"¡Salúd!"

KHADIJA sipped a water she had quietly poured earlier.

We smoked a little pinner, 21 Savage was on the speakers. They were good speakers, worth a few hundred bucks, well-wrought.

At a certain point Medina turned to me and said, "do u take Khadija X to be ur wife?"

"Yeah, f'sho, O.K."

She turned to Khadija, "do u take Muhammad X to be ur husband?"

"Yes."

We rolled around Los Angeles for a couple hours, stoned off medicinal grade THC edibles and Cannabis tincture in a black 2014 Mustang convertible we found ourselves in the acquisition of, listening to a Bloodstone's Greatest Hits CD we had copped at a gas station.

We checked into The Standard, penthouse suite. We took a shower, smashed, took another shower, smashed again, took another shower. We got steaks and mimosas from room service, watched The Misfits. Marilyn Monroe and Cary Grant. Written by her husband Arthur Miller. Tight movie.

Cary Grant was doing LSD psychotherapy thru-out the filming and u could tell, his acting was super vivid. Marilyn, of course, always did her thing.

"I'm pregnant."

"Mashallah."

2.

"It's bigger than Hip Hop mane."

I sprinkled psylocibin 'shrooms on my taco while MULLAH X soap boxed:

"EZEKIEL SAW THE WHEEL WAY UP IN THE MIDDLE OF THE AIR. THERE WAS A WHEEL WITHIN THE WHEEL. THERE WAS A FACE MADE OF FOUR MEN, THE RIGHT SIDE OF THE FACE WAS A MAN WHO WAS AN OX, WHICH SYMBOLIZES STRENGTH. THE LEFT SIDE OF THE FACE WAS MADE OF A MAN WHO WAS A LION, WHICH REPRESENTS COURAGE. IT IS STRENGTH AND COURAGE THAT WE NEED TO PROCEED AND ACHIEVE FREEDOM. TAKE 2% MILK, WHAT'S THE OTHER 98%? AND WHY IS MILK WHITE? ANOTHER DEVIL TRICK. THE WHEEL WITHIN THE WHEEL IS THE MOTHER PLANE PROPHESIED TO APPROACH AT THE HOUR OF FINAL JUDGEMENT. A PLANE BOTH PHYSICAL AND SPIRITUAL."

He was right. We were in a large abandoned auto body shop in West Oakland. There were maybe 20, 30 pianos stored in the back, upright, grand, baby grand, a couple of them were like 100 years old.

The taco was carne asada from the truck down the block. It was a good taco, I barely tasted the shrooms.

I washed it down with a Pacifico.

"ASTAGHFIRULLAH!"

"ASTAGHFIRULLAH"

"ASTAGHFIRULLAH! LA ILLAHA ILLALLAH, MUHAMMADUN RASULULLAH!"

"ASTAGHFIRULLAH! LA ILLAHA ILLALLAH, MUHAMMADUN RASULULLAH!"

"ALLAH!"

"ALLAH!"

"ELLEGUAH!"

"ELLEGUAH!"

"YEMAYA! YEMAYA!"

"YEMAYA! YEMAYA!"

"ALLAH!"

"ALLAH!"

"CHANGO!"

"CHANGO!"

"JAH RASTAFARI!"

"JAH RASTAFARI!"

"OM"

"OM"

"WOW!"

"WOW!"

"OH!"

"OH!"

I called up Khadija, "Ay slide thru, I'm at our fourth wedding."

She was there in 20 minutes, just came from the nail shop, she had long on emerald green nails, was driving a matching emerald green 1969 Corvette Stingray, stepped out the whip with a chilled bottle of Moët Chandon in her hand.

"Nice venue."

I caught her up: "There's like 50 pianos back there, couple of em like 100 years old."

She sat on the couch, brought out a mirror and vial of coke, cut a line for me, popped the bottle poured some bubbly for ur boy.

The coke was actually very good.

She, pregnant, abstained.

MULLAH X spake:

"CHAMPAGNE AND COCAINE ARE PLEASANT FOR THE OCCASIONAL HOBBY BUT ULTIMATELY USELESS IN COMPARISON WITH ALLAH, THAT'S WHY I'M STICKING TO ONE LINE OF COCAINE AND ONE GLASS OF CHAMPAGNE ON THIS VERY SPECIAL ONCE IN A LIFETIME OCCASION AND I SUGGEST U DO TOO. WE CAN DO A FOLLOW UP WEDDING LATER IN A PROPER MOSQUE WITH NO DRINK BUT FOR NOW THIS IS THE REAL ONE. BOTH OF YAL REPEAT AFTER ME: ALLAH!"

"ALLAH!"

"JAH RASTAFARI!"

"JAH RASTAFARI!"

"YEMAYA! YEMAYA!"

"YEMAYA! YEMAYA!"

"CHANGO!"

"CHANGO!"

"YEMAYA!"
"YEMAYA!"
"ALLAH!"
"ALLAH!"
"YEMAYA! YEMAYA!"
"YEMAYA! YEMAYA!"
"NOW KISS!"

We did. We stuck around for a minute bullshitting listening to Thin Lizzy, finished the champagne, cracked into some beers, finished the coke. Khadija, pregnant, abstained.

"Peace."

"Peace my brutha."

"See u later."

We peeled out, swung by the Black and White for a 5th of Henny and went to go see Memorias del Subdesarollo over at the Emery Bay United Artists Theatre.

Tight flick. Swam back to the pad in Paradise Hills, threw on a Bud Powell record, had some calm sideways relations. Listened to a Santana record drinking tea and smoking a doobie. Some more tender caresses and a deep sleep.

3.

"I'm the best rapper," I whispered into the void of the night and the void howled back: "No doubt, no doubt."

I was in Berlin somewhere by the wall, I can't remember which side, I was off some Molly and had been drinking and then I had smoked some DMT and went off walking, I felt dimensions falling away from me like the shedding of skins.

Gounod's Faust was playing.

The void said:

"Nel mezzo del cammin di nostra vita

Mi ritroval per una selva oscura

Ché la diritta era smarrita."

Or maybe I did, what's the difference, am I right?

As the DMT wore off, I realized I wasn't listening to Gounod's Faust I was listening to "There Will Never Be Another You" by Bud Powell, and I wasn't in Berlin, I was in Khadija's Bedstuy apartment, lying on the bed. The head game was that crazy. The apartment was in the attic of a Catholic Church. Our Lady of Victory on Throop. She started reading 1001 Arabian Nights out loud to me but then we got bored and she rolled some Blue Dream into fronto leaf for me and poured me some Pinot Grigio. I smoked my little blunt and drank my little wine and we watched 2001: A Space Odyssey on a 110 inch flatscreen TV with my hand on her stomach, lil baby pulling itself together in there.

After the movie I put on a Ray Charles record that just said Ray Charles on it with a picture of Ray Charles. Beautiful record.

Khadija flipped idly thru the Kama Sutra for a bit and then we spiritually congressed. Rain fell. Khadija made some tea. I smoked another fronto blunt and we drank tea watching the rain.

4.

We was riding dirty down the 1, me and Khadija in a white 1999 Acura Legend, with Khadija listening to the new Project Pat tape. We were somewhere between weed country and wine country.

She asked me who Albert Einstein was.

"What do u mean, who's Albert Einstein?"

"Who is he? I don't know."

"He was a German mathematician, or like physicist I guess? E = mc 2. Energy equals mass times the speed of light squared. Theory of Relativity."

"Did he build the Atomic Bomb?"

"Naw, but his theoretical work led to it I guess."

Highway patrol car rolled up behind us and whooped its siren, flashed its lights. We pulled over.

Copper walked up to the window.

"Do u know why I pulled you over?"

"No, why?"

"I wanted to inform you that Albert Einstein signed a letter to President Roosevelt lobbying for the creation of the atom bomb. And this letter was said to be highly influential in Roosevelt's decision to sign off on the Manhattan Project."

"No shit?"

A seagull landed on our hood and interjected: "Yeah but he was only doing it to beat the Nazis and later he said it was his life's one regret."

I mulled it over.

"Hmm... Seems like Einstein was O.K."

Khadija was less than convinced, "whoever he was, he seems insignificant."

"Who isn't?" Said the seagull and flew off.

The cop drew his six shooter and said, "Ur under arrest u stinkin varmint, get outa the car and lie down on the ground, braid ur fingers behind ur head, u stay in the car for now ma'am."

I did as I was told. Heard seven shots and saw the copper's body fall down dead next to mine. My beautiful bride had shot seven holes in the porker and they were all leaking blood now.

We we hopped back in the carriage, skreeked off and parked at the next beach we saw, swam out to Hawaii. A friend put us up in a house while the heat died down. For days we swam all day, ate swordfish steaks and drank beer all night listening to Miles Davis' Sketches of Spain on repeat.

It was a good time but eventually we had to head back to the yay. Paradise Hills was home now and home was calling.

5.

We were posted up at the crib, I was blowing that woop, listening to a Paul Butterfield Blues Band record I had found in a junk shop up in Crescent City.

Khadija's girl Afrooz with the hand tats rolled thru, brought some wax and a rig, we dabbed and listened to Curtis Mayfield.

I swirled off into my own thoughts while they pontificated on various concepts of reality.

At a certain point, mid pontification, Afrooz turned to me and said, "Do u take Khadija to be ur wife?"

"Yeah."

She turned to Khadija and asked her if she took me to be her husband.

"Fsho."

"Swag, turn up then."

I kissed my bride, poured some red wine for me and Afrooz and we all smoked some shisha. Khadija, with child, had a token puff then abstained.

We hopped into Afrooz's Wraith and whipped around Paradise Hills bumpin Thugger. A thick white heavy fog enveloped the tree lined skreets and the skreet lamps cast an eerie glow on the whole suburban scene.

We pulled up to a Jack in the Box drive thru and ordered 3 large ice teas. We drove down to Pill Hill and I dipped into the Walgreen's, ran into a famous alt lit writer picking up his scrips. He had thrown out his back so on top of his usual adderalls and xans, he had some oxies. He sprinkled a handful of pills like Skittles into my hand and I tossed them back, washed them down with a Cucumber Gatorade I had picked up in aisle 7. I bid him adieu, snatched a disposable camera and bounced without paying.

The Wraith scraped off as the Walgreen rent-a-cop fired some lazy rounds off at us.

Afrooz was salty: "Bruh u got bullet holes in my new Wraith."

"I know an auto body shop that can take care of that they owe me a favor."

"U a fool," my wife told me.

We drove to Treasure Island and took 27 disposable photos of the moon, headed back to the Walgreen's to drop off the camera.

The Walgreen rent-a-cop stood up when I walked in, ice grilled ur boy, fired some intimidation shots into the ceiling, bits of particle board trickled down like sleet. The manager Chuck who I was cool with was there now he said, "Hey! Cool it soldier!" The Walgreen rent-a-cop sat back down.

I dropped the disposable camera with the 1 hour photo developer, a yung azn grrl. Name tag said Joy. She gave me smile and I returned the sentiment.

We whipped down the skreet and killed an hour taking Soju shots at the late nite Korean spot. My beautiful bride, in a family way, of course abstained, maybe a sip of Soju for symbolism. We all picked slowly at a kimchi scallion pancake. When an hour was up we hit the 'greens to pick up our photos.

Flipping thru the stack in the parking lot I noticed that instead of 27 pictures of the moon, it was 26 pictures of the sun. I hopped back out the whip and went back in there.

"Joy, this is 26 pictures of the sun. I took 27 pictures of the moon."

"U gave me the negatives, the positives are inverted. The opposite of the moon is the sun."

It added up.

"How do u account for the missing photo?"

"That's just how those cameras go. Sometimes that last picture doesn't snap."

"I would like a partial refund."

She popped open the register and handed me 3 shiny new pennies.

"Thanks ma."

These pennies were lucky I could tell, I told Afrooz roll down to the liquor store so I could buy us 3 scratchers.

Scooped dem, scratched dem with our lucky pennies. Won a hunnit clams each. Ran back into the store and copped 300 tall cans of Arizona. Ordered them to be delivered to one of the trap houses down in Fremont.

The sun was up.

We stopped into the Koffee Pot, got coffees, split up the disposable sun photos as follows: 12 for Afrooz, 7 for Khadija, 7 for me. Afrooz dropped us back at the crib. We had some coffee, I smoked a cig on the balcony. We had a lazy smash and fell asleep.

6.

We were posted at the crib in Paradise Hills, listening to Vincentico Valdez con las Sonora Matancera. I was sipping a Pinot noir, regal, poised, pensive. Felt like Ice Cube narrating a documentary on Eames. Felt like the human version of Prodigy's audio-book memoir. I felt like a Cuban Mac Dre, swaggy, thinky, Hemingway-esqe. I was probably high off drugs, I coulda been high off the Holy Ghost, Allah, et al., what's the diff?

The cops had just shot another unarmed black kid and heads were gathering in downtown Oakland. Khadija's mom was over for tea. They were somberly chirping in Farsi.

I dipped out and drove the gold '99 Sebring over to Chinatown, parked and walked over to by the cop station where maybe a couple hundred cops in riot gear (shields, batons, helmets, body armor, tasers, tear gas grenades, rubber bullet cannons, pistols, shotguns, rifles, etc.) stood facing a couple hundred protestors and onlookers (cameras, phone cameras, signs, guitars, drums, stereos, megaphones, a couple scattered bonfires).

A cop on a megaphone was saying "Disperse!" and a random dude in the crowd on a megaphone was saying "Fuck you!" I watched the back and forth ensue for several minutes:

"DISPERSE!"

"FUCK YOU!"

"DISPERSE!"

"FUCK YOU!"

And so on, cops lined up on one end of the block, people crowded on the other end, both frozen with a strange awkward reluctance.

I walked down the block past a couple fires, a drugstore had been busted into and people were running in and running out with various prizes. I went in, got a Tecate and a pack of Kools, went and watched a fire in the intersection of like 10th and Broadway. The vibe over here was more mellow and cheerful. No cops. Saw a couple of the homies, said what up. Went over to a bar for a couple drinks, cut.

Hopped in the whipper, trotted home, stopped at the 7-11 for a pint of coffee ice cream for the wife. It was one of her few indulgences.

Pulled up to the crib and ducked back in, mother in law was asleep on the couch, some Korean soap opera going, she was into the Korean soaps lately.

Khadija was sleeping in the bedroom, I slipped in next to her and rubbed the baby bump, drifted off.

The protests continued over the next couple days and throughout the course of the year and onward. The cops, continuing their tradition, went on to murder upwards of a thousand unarmed black men, women and children without repercussion, and consistently, like clockwork, employed illegal and excessive force on outraged protestors. An ancient script, enough to make a younger player want to up and move down Mexico way or some such.

7.

I came into possession of a half gallon of liquid acid for an outrageous price I think it came out to like 50 cents a hit. Basically free money and I was looking for a couple retailers to take some of it off of my hands.

I ended up drinking at an old haunt with an even older compadre I hadn't seen in years.

"Been a while mane."

"Fsho. How's Mike?"

"Mike's dead."

"Damn, how?"

"Speedball."

"Wow."

"I know."

"How's Lucky?"
"He's dead too."
"For real? How?"
"Shot."
"Wow."
We sat for a minute drinking our beers.
I told the bartender 3 shots of Patrón, he poured them and I gave him one.
"I'm working."
"Two of our friends are dead, come on."
"OK."
"¡Salúd!"
Bartender scooted off and we resumed our business.
"So how's 7 per, that's more than fair."
"5."
"6."
"OK."
He took it all, I didn't even have to call my other dude. I had set aside enough for personal use of course. In fact I was high off it at that very moment and it was true professional shit. Everything was glowing and breathing, I was taking long blinks and seeing fireworks in my brain but everything felt super clear and fearless.
Mike, it made sense he was dead. He loved speed balling. I don't blame him, speed balling feels great. Lucky was kinda unexpected. Thought about Lucky. Not so lucky no more, huh? Or maybe he was. Maybe the next level is far superior. Let's hope.
"Man, Lucky."
"I know man."
"Is the next level superior?"
"Huh?"

"Is death OK?"
"Death is nothing."
"Is life better than death?"
"Life is better than nothing, yeah."
"So there's nothing to look forward to?"
"No, I guess not."
"But there's nothing to fear then either tho, right?"
"Yeah, probably not."
"Tight, tight, that's what's up."
"Groovy, mane."
"No doubt."

8.

"Zen, zen, zen, zen, zen, zen, zen, zen, zen, zen, zen, zen, zen, zen, zen, zen, zen, zen, zen, zen, zen."

I had dropped a little too much of that LSD, was in a state of metanoic reverie, couldn't see a way out apart from saying:

"Zen, zen, zen, zen, zen, zen, zen, zen, zen, zen, zen, zen, zen, zen, zen, zen, zen, zen, zen, zen, zen."

A few minutes or seconds or hours or days or whatever passed and the metanoia loosened its vice grip, the compulsory mantra petered out. I was brite n clear again.

Khadija was taking a nap. I went out for a rare walk thru Paradise Hills. Birds were out tweeting. Felt ordered, harmonious. The sunlight was humming, cosmic, musical.

A warm glow brimmed from my frame. My legs felt strong, they propelled me forward like I was sitting on two ferocious dogs. My lungs breathed in that suburban mountain air.

A deer sprang forth in front of me and planted his hooves, looked at ur boy. Big male buck, looked a lot like old Changey but with an entire four legged body attached to his neck. Poor Changey, just hanging there on Medina's wall, only the occasional shot of mescal to calm his nerves. But he took it all in stride. Brave and beautiful soul.

Then I realized, this WAS Changey.

"Changey mane."

"Ya Soy CHANGO."

"CHANGO!"

Chango, radiant, en su forma final.

A doe trotted after Chango and posed behind him, may-haps Yemaya, then two more does, Oshun and Yemoja, who looked to be preggers. Regardless, a swaggy Squad. Some wild turkeys squawked and swooped down from a low hanging branch of a local tree, joined the squad. A sleepy raccoon strolled up, joined the team. A possum and her child walked up, jumped in on the action.

The phalanx of woodland creatures stood there flanking young Chango in the middle of the street staring at ur boy with their deep, dark animal eyes, brimming with pathos and wisdom. We all stood like that for quite some time, felt like a joyous century. Then a Toyota Corolla rolled up and they scattered. I continued on my walk.

A hawk skreeked and soared above, observing, guarding, blessing the path. I was thankful for him.

"I'm thankful for u brother," I called up to the hawk.

"No doubt, no doubt," the hawk squawked back.

12 white doves landed on a parked cop car.

"Sup ladies."
They all said at the same time: "Hola."
"K paso"
"Nada, tu"
"Nado"
I was feeling chèvre.
I found a cigarette behind my ear and lit it, flexed my muscles.
"K macho" said one of the palomas
"Ay mami"
"Ay Ay Ay" sez Paloma.
Y nada fue la misma...
The 12 doves all took single solitary all white, perfectly circular boo boos on the yop car and flew into the blue black sun. The White Doves were Black. Las Palomas Blancas estaban Negras, in other words. The blu blk sun shone, real.

9.

We were cruising thru the night in Paradise Hills, moving thru hues of light, white and yellow lamps piercing thru trees and ivies and whatnot, white moon glowing behind powdery blue clouds, casting a wavy glow across the cool dark midnight blue air, wild radiant.

The song on the radio was like "this ones for love and affection," and it was tru...

The whipper was a stolen Dodge Charger, matte black, 2013 or 14 maybe, pink dice on the rear view, came like that, they looked funny, I left them there.

Khadija took the aux cord and put on "Most Power Full Lakshmi" by Gayathri Mantram. We drove around the suburbs of Heaven: South Kensington, Northwest Kensington, San Pablo, Santa Fauna, Santa Dymphna Real, SIr Francis Drake Boulevard Houses, Oakville Cricus, San Rafael, Rodeo City, Sausalito, the Marin Headlands, Truckee South, Marin Proper, Forestville, the V, Hillside, Concord, Hercules, Moraga, WSO/NSO/ESO, the dubs specific, Brookfield, BVHP, the BVs, La Lima, the Dirty, Murder Hill Canyon, Lafayette, Lafayette Del Norte, Diablo Valley, Walnut Creek, Perla Rara, and of course: Paradise Hill.

I recalibrated my consciousness using highly futuristic spiritualities and changed the paint job on the Charger from Black to Blue.

Commercial came on for Adderall.

"What else, DJ?"

She played a song called: "Lord Shiva most powerful mantra, warning"

Apparently 200 million people had listened to it on YouTube. Raver music basically I guess.

The streets were completely empty except for us.

I sped up a little, hit the corners with a modicum of style.

I was hella stoned, thinking shallow thoughts that felt deep. The difference between shallow and deep felt negligible.

Put on some of the ol' om shrimrim sarasvatyenamaha n' the wife went into deep meditation.

After that I threw on some "There Will Never Be a Better U" by Bud Powell, wrote a book.

It was a novel I called it Peyote Karaoke it was gona get published but Khadija shot me a glance and I rewrote it, published the newer version instead. Peyote Karaoke disappeared from the past and present and sat forever in the future.

Now that the book had come out we were rich and driving around Paradise Hills in a Midnite Blue Charger of recent vintage.

"We oughta move to Mexico"

"O.K."

10.

"Maybe I'm doing too much," I was singing along to my own song thinking about how much of a musical genius I was.

We were crossing the border with a little tree no big deal it's legal now. We got waved thru.

Ended up in Santa Sirena.

Rented a little house off a dirt road on a cliff overlooking the sea.

Decided to just post up there for the year, maybe forever. Some business came up after a couple months tho and we headed back to Paradise Hills.

"But hold the spot" we told dude, his name was Mickey.

Mickey said: "O.K."

"No doubt. Thanks Mickey."

"No prob."

"Ur our landlord now Mickey, can u handle that responsibility?"

"Of course, as long as rent slides thru on a regular basis."

"Rent is theft."

"U right."

We left it at that. I decided right there I didn't need to pay rent. I guess I had decided that long ago. Some ideas are older than actual people mane, that's crazy to me.

So there we were back at the spot in Paradise Hills, plotting the move to Santa Sirena. It was like 6 bedrooms in the Paradise Hills spot, ill lil spot. So, being that the house was large, Khadija's sister Malika, a lawyer, and her dude Marty, a surfer, were lamping there too, and a cousin, his name was Ali Ala, he made a lot of money off computers somehow. He was a cool party dude, liked to drink, banker type, math guy.

He poured me a gin and tonic and said:

"I got a good idea: PHARMA BUMS"

That was a good idea.

"That is a good idea."

We drank some more, me, Ali Ala and Marty.

I think the democrat debate was going on TV, The Lesser Evils Show, as it were.

Switched to egg nog, it was that time of year.

Arthur Lee's band called Love was playing. I was off a brownie.

A fight was recounted. We were all drunk and high except my bride who, with child, abstained.

We talked about the future of the peso.

Off screen, a live studio audience laffed, weeped, guffawed at all the appropriate moments.

The wives went and reclined upstairs.

A nice sauce was simmering.

Another egg nog. It actually went hard.

I felt like Ernest Hemingway again.

Somebody mentioned the Kennedys.

Dracula: Dead and Loving It came on TV.

Ali Ala had the remote. He flipped the channel again, the Warriors beat the Thunder.

Turned off the TV and listened to the same three Love records we had just listened to again but this time without the TV.

Khadija and Malika, who had fallen asleep in their respective couches upstairs, woke up, retired to their respective beds.

We ate without them, it was like 10 or 11, little late for dinner, they woke up a little later and snacked on leftovers.

Went upstairs, threw on Wes Montgomery's Tequila and danced with my wife, her belly was big, there was a kid in there.

11.

(Philly Joe Jones Solo)

I spit some Havana Club out the front window pa mi primo and lit a San Lazaro candela pa mi salúd.

It was the best of times, it was the worst of times. It was the combination best of times and worst of times.

Khadija prepared some auga pa chocolate, it was hella caliente. I took a siesta. Cuando llevé, estabamos listo pa una fiesta. Had some snugglers, that's Mexican hot chocolate with peppermint Schnapps. It was R.L. Burnside on the system now. Everybody was grinnin.

Ate some meatloaf, drank some beer, felt super sleepily American, that is to say, weak.

Another sweet dinner in Paradise Hills with my glowing, expecting bride Khadija X, her sister rich expert lawyer, Malika, pro surfer Marty Martinez, and Ali Ala, lovable tech bro.

Turned on the TV, Wolf on Wall Skreet.

A police chopper buzzed overhead like a super harsh mosquito of death.

Some whisky was poured, hecka skrong.

Somebody said: "Why is it that the Christmas Tree is the Death Star?" Shit, might have even been me.

"Miles Davis, Santana."

"ALLAH, CHANGO, JAH RASTAFARI."

The conversation turned into a baklava and we each ate a square. Another Arabian Nite.

I dipped out, hit the Indian Casino up the street, won a hundred at the ten dollar blackjack table. I was beginning to imagine myself there all night so I quit while I was up and went to the 7/11 to buy some ice cream. Won ten bucks off a scratcher there, I was on a roll.

Drove over to the Hotsy Totsy, spraypainted "KILL WHITEY" over the confederate flag they had hanging in the window.

Then I went over to the Ivy Room ordered a shot of Makers, drank that and walked out, jumped back into the whip (which one was it? The Silver '77 Buick Riviera? Think so. Oh word yeah, I was right) and smobbishly slumped dolo around town.

The Philly Joe Jones drum solo was going from the beginning of the chapter.

Here we are: Chapter 11, Knowledge Knowledge. Knowledge of Knowledge. One cipher complete, the second spin of the wheel. The wheel within the wheel, way up in the air, the mother plane.

I looked up in the sky and saw it there, the wheel, within the wheel, the mother plane, the black star, the black sun, coming for to carry me home.

I died and went to Heaven.

Here I was whipping the Silver Gawd Gawd thru downtown Heaven.

I thought: Damn how long is this drum solo? It was still going.

12.

I was at the Medici in Hyde Park, down over Chi-raq way, drinking a glass of dark rum slowly watching Philly Joe Jones, still soloing from the last chapter with five of my cousins and my aunt and uncle. I caught a ride from one of my cousins to a the hotel downtown where I was staying and I posted up there waiting for Rajlukshmee Debee Bhattachary from Al Jazeera come interview me.

My suite doorbell rang, I answered it, she came in with a white British camera man, camera rolling. She held up a sambo doll in blue and and sambo doll in red, and said, "I'd like u to answer a few questions."

Gounod's Faust was playing but as I creened my ear, on closer inspection, it was actually the Ray Charles song, "Misery in my Heart."

And I realized I was in The Hague, Netherlands.

Rajlukshmee Debee Bhattachary peeled off her face (a remarkably well made latex mask) to reveal that she was in fact Netherland High Council Criminal Justice Nastja van Strien.

"Who are you?"

"Wait, who said that, me or you?"

"I don't know."

"O.K."

All of a sudden, I was in handcuffs and an orange jumpsuit. I thought, "this is no good," and recalibrated my conscious reality using highly futuristic spiritual techniques and woke up in Bedstuy with Khadija X. As the furniture slid into focus I realized it wasn't Bedstuy but Paradise Hills. Of course.

I had fallen asleep on the couch. Ali Ala was asleep on the other couch. Marty Martinez was awake on the other couch watching a cartoon. Malika was off asleep in her bedroom and Khadija was just walking down from upstairs where she had been in deep meditation for hours, painstakingly creating every aspect of my reality. She curled up next to me.

Took a shot from a 100 dollar bottle of whiskey Marty had acquired for free. Was smooth.

Looked at the cartoon on TV.

A cute duck said: "Reality is a deadly game."

A cute bunny said: "Life is death."

A cute mouse said: "Death is life."

"What's this show called?"

"Animal Friends."

Ali Ala woke up and started talking about the stability of gold in the global market and then he talked about real estate for a long time. We all listened while Marty flipped the channels.

"Bismuth is experiencing a price spike right now," I offered.

"Bismuth?" Ali Ala asked.

Khadija X said: "It's a heavy metal. weakly radioactive, a lot of psychic properties."

"I'll buy some," Ali Ala decided.

He sent a text.

"Give me some ideas, I'm up right now."

"Just stick with the Bismuth one for a while, meditate on that one," I told him.

Khadija X reached into the folds of her white gown and found a small circle of freshly smelted Bismuth, oxidized (or alchemized or burnt with fire or however they do) into a beautiful iridescent rainbow color (powerful stuff), proffered it to Ali Ala.

"I'm gonna be a millionaire!" he sighed with wonder.

"U already are, baby!" I told him.

13.

I was at La Botanica Ramajuel out in Richmond, parked in the lot in a Dodge Ram Wagon. There were some box Chevies and a couple Lincolns, there was a function going on in or around these parts starting nowish. Everybody was geared up. We were hotboxing the van with a hashish dutchy, it was me, Riffs McGriff, Lil Carlito, Big Maf, and The Dangler. The Dangler was sitting out the cypher but still catching a heady contact blit.

We had cracked some Tecates, we were waiting on some tacos.

Maf: "How bout them Warriors?"

The Dangler: "Warriors mane."

Riffs: "Warriors mane."

Me: "They got ur Spurs this year, Carlito."

Carlito was from San Anto, naturally he was salty.

"!Ay! Yo se. Pinche Warriors guey. Just remember we got u two years ago cabrón."

"U right but I'm talking about right now, mane."

Buzzcocks tape was in there, warbling around, we were hearing the tape's energy radiate thru the air, electrical.

"What's he saying here? How's the hook go?" I asked.

"They're saying, 'Everybody's coming on my neck."

Ew.

"Pretty sure that's not what they're saying."

We sat and listened for a second. It actually did sound like he was saying "Everybody's coming on my neck." Naw. Couldn't be. We listened for the hook again.

"It's 'Everybody's happy nowadays.'"

"See? I was close."

Our tacos were up. Stepped out the van like Cheech and Chong + 3, went and sat at a table with our tacos and beers.

It was sunny. Felt nice.

"Mane, I just realized I'm hella high."

"Me too."

"Shit I'm high and I ain't even smoke."

"Bruh, it's a trip how u can smoke weed hella times and each time u still get high."

"Huh yeah, seems like it oughta just stop working, right?"

"Yeah but then, why would it?"

"Why would anything?"

"True."

Rare, legendary conversation.

"Mane, where Joe Joe?"

"New York."

"Oh yeah."

"Damn ur hella high."

"I'm sayin."

We finished our beers and our tacos, screeped out.

We listened to Social Unrest.

"Wow, this band is hella good."

"Yeah."

Ended up on the roof of the abandoned grocery store where Riffs lived, drinking beers and smoking weed and hash out of a bong, listening to Dead Kennedys.

Binny Shrimpboy, Skinhead Scoot, Rico, Jay Jay, Brent and Miguelito were there too, it was an expansive roof with multiple couches.

Carlito talked about moving to the area from Tejas & Jay Jay rattled off some obscure musical trivia while everybody listened, sometimes rolling a joint or a cigarette, sometimes getting up for a beer or a coffee or a tea.

There were 3 women in the building: Mahadevi, Gladys & Knife Girl, but they were on straw mats in states of deep meditation, quietly calculating and orchestrating the thoughts and movements of every male body in there from now into perpetuity. It was a highly spiritual port of congress.

I called up Khadija: "Slide thru, it's our fifth wedding."

"Sixth," she said and hung up, was there in 15, fresh from the nail shop, pink nails and a pink Lambo with the doors that open upwards like Back 2 Tha Future.

She came in, Riffs offered her a seat, she politely declined and instead unrolled two prayer rugs, sat on one. I joined her.

Mullah X Parachuted from the sky to read us our rites:

"U HAVE THE RITE 2 LUV & B LUVED. LET THERE B LITE. WHERE THERE B LITE THERE BEE DEE LITE. LIVE LUV LAFF. ALLAH!"

"ALLAH!"

"U MAY NOW KISS THE BRIDE MY BRUTHA!"

We smooched.

Jay Jay resumed his musical trivia ticker tape parade mantra and we all sat entranced.

14.

Khadija's water broke out in Perla Rara as we were strolling thru a botanical garden. We hopped in the Sebring and slid over to Perla Rara hospital, very nice spot, there was a grand piano and an atrium in the entryway.

They brought us to a swimming pool on the roof and we stripped naked and dived in. The baby slid out like a dolphin. We lifted her from the water and I bit her umbilical cord off, held her to the sun. Cute lil creature.

We named her Fatima X.

We lounged poolside with some mojitos (virgin for Fatima), drying off in the sun. It was a beautiful day.

A nurse brought the three of us matching Gucci tracksuits and escorted us to the waiting chopper on the H pad.

We were helicoptered back to the crib in Paradise Hills and began the childrearing process. The baby was great, all its parts worked, it gurgled and cooed and sipped milk from its mama's teat, then fell asleep.

The next morning we woke up and the baby had two cups of coffee for us like, "what we on today patna."

Decided to take her to the Paradise Hills Museum of Modern Art. They had a Martín Ramirez exhibit up and their permanent collection was decent: Hopper, Picasso, Dali, Guston, Diebenkorn, Pollock, O'Keefe, Bourgeois, Haring.

She loved Martín Ramirez, Bourgeois and O'Keefe. The other ones I'd figure she'd dig later. They needed some better Picassos. There was a Sol Lewitt that caught her attention, had her scratching her chin. And she dug the lil Cy Twombly they had goin'.

As we left she yawned, "Hardly modern now was it?"

And I had to agree.

I bought her an easel, some canvases and a stand, she did a moody abstract expressionist series. I called up a dealer I know and got her a solo show in SOMA. She was literally born yesterday but she was on her way.

The show opening went off pretty well, most of the works sold, and a handful of noteworthy collectors, Gallerists from France, Italy and Spain left their cards and insisted I call them as soon as convenient.

"What's next?" we asked young Fatima X.

"Sculpture."

15.

I was in a hot tub with my beautiful bride Khadija X, Mashallah, Allah Hu Akbar, Allah.

Malika was watching Fatima. When we left them, they were reading the Q'ran together.

Paradise Hills had a nice little bath house with outdoor cedar hot tubs. We had each rolled up a joint of YURPLE MUHAMMAD X, a new strain some farmers I knew up north had made and named in honor of urs true.

It was powerful skrong, fragrant, body and head highs, sleepy yet upful, euphoric.

It was quiet, except for the tub burbling and the occasional nite bird chirping.

Beautiful clear night.

We sat there in that silence for 3 hours.

When u listen to silence for a long time, it gets pretty loud.

It starts with that burble and that nite bird chirp then stretches out to the rustling of tree leaves, faint noises of traffic in the distance, this or that footstep, the creak of a wooden structure, the sound of u own breathing and the breathing of the woman across from u, heartbeats, even, fuck I mean even in a quiet room there's the expanding of the lungs and the beating of the fucking human heart, those things get loud as fuck. So throw a hot tub motor in there, the heater, the lil bufador shooting the bubbles, the gentle lapping of the waters on the wood or what have u, that's a deafeningly loud silence. It's huge and beautiful to listen to. It's quite lovely.

We left and hit Ya Ya Vegan Japanese Restaurant, got a Paradise Roll: avocado, cucumber, carrot, daikon, pickled ginger in rice, wrapped in seaweed, sprinkled with sesame. She got a tea, I got a water, a tea and a beer (the top three beverages on earth, in that order)

I came clean: "One thing I don't like about you is u force me to spiritually box with u constantly. What's worse tho is u force me to work in front of u so u can steal all my styles and swaggy secrets."

"No doubt"

"Oh word?"

"Word."

"O.K."

"Word O.K."

"What are we talking about?"

"Who knows?"

Dang this Yurple Muhammad X strain went hard, I was going to have a time living up to it.

"Everything is trill."

"U do everything for urself."

"So do u."

"Ur useless."

"Who cares?"

"What is care?"

"Prove to me ur mere mortal flesh."

"Why should flesh be mortal."

"Alack, Alee!"

"ALLAH"

Extreme Romance Is Essentially Warfare, Espionage, Bricolage, Recon, Hustle, A good D, pivot, metalurgy, strength, tenacity…

The phone rang, was my sister Munda:

"Sup brah."

"Just shreddin the gnar."

"Thaswasup, ay give me a ride to this party."

"Fsho, hold up… Ay we gota give Munda a ride."

"O.K."

Drove over to Munda's crib, scooped her, "where to?"

"Fillmoe."

"Damn Malika with the baby tho."

"She got it, that baby can handle her own damn self anyways."

"Word O.K."

It was more Hayes Valley than Fillmore tbh.

"Come in for a minute."

"O.K."

Wine. Abraxis. Candles, incense, it was her homie Suena crib.

"Oh u aint tell me it was Suena house."

"Fuck outa here nigga I aint even knew yal knew each other"

Suena and me had a shot of Patron and cracked beers. She had a bowl of limes already cut, a methodical and practical woman. Munda and Khadija drank water."

I noticed A Clockwork Orange was on TV, a weird choice but I was fuckin widdit.

It was like 10 other folks there, the four of us sat on the sofa and talked about astrology, had another round of beers.

I leaned over to my beautiful bride Khadija and whispered into her ear, "Fillmoe."

She kissed my neck.

We hung around for a bit then cut back to Paradise Hills. Malika and Fatima were watching Aristocats, one of Fatima's favorites.

I asked Fatima: "How was it?"

She said: "Lit."

She seemed to be telling the truth.

Malika said: "Hey it's the solstice."

She's a lawyer so she should know. She's also Persian so that's two reasons.

Arezoo and Asa swooped thru Arezoo was an actress and Asa, I forgot what she did but she was with a white dude with glasses and money, local dude from the neighborhood, he did his thing.

Asa and Arezoo cracked open pomegranates and started filling a big gold bowl with them. The bowl was real gold, it looked crazy.

Khadija cracked a pomegranate and got to it too. I got myself some tea, which Malika had brewed, and she cracked a pom and started filling the bowl too. Marty came home.

"Sup Marty."

"Sup mane."

I went on the back porch with Marty and smoked a hash joint. He had built the back porch himself. Marty Martinez, good dude.

Went inside, smoked hookah, hashish, opium, more hookah, drank hella tea, ate hella pomegranate seeds (smackin), deposited our concerns, anxieties and inhibitions into the spiritual urn of the mind and fully revolved reality into its current state in which u, dear reader, find urself.

Anyway, peace, see u in chapter 16.

16.

I was en El Studio on Napoleon in San Francisco, laying some fire bars down on wax:

ESTABA POESIANDO
CHA CHA CHA
OOH BABY BABY
OOOH MAMA
BOOM SHAKA LAKA
AYAYAYAY
CANTA NO LLORES
PORQUE CANTANDO SE ALLEGRA
CIELITO LINDO
SHOOP DOOBIE DOOBIE DOO
WOW
ALLAH
YEMAYA
CHANGO
JAH RASTA

BOOM BOOM
BANG BANG
ZIP ZOOM ZAGGA ZOW
ZIG ZAG ZIG ALLAH
PEACE ALLAH JAH JAH
YAWEH JESUCRISTO
SIETE POTENCIAS AFRICANAS
BASO D'AGUA
BABALU AYE
ELLEGUA ACHE
OSHUN OSUN OLORUN AYE
BIDDY BIDDY BOM BOM BUYAKA
BUYAKA
BRING IT STR8 2 YA
ZIPPY DEE DOO DAH
DOO WA DIDDY
HIPPY TO THE HOPPY
U DONT STOP THE ROCKITY ROCKITY ROCK
    ROCKITY REE
WOP BABALUBOP BUHLOPLAMLOO
NUTHIN BUT PIMPS AND PLAYERS IN THE
    YAYAY REAL LIFE SLANGING YAYAY
BLING BLING EVERYTIME I COME AROUND
    UR CITY BLING BLING
I KNOW WHEN THAT HOTLINE BLING
THAT COULD ONLY MEAN ONE TING FURL
    MEH
YABBA DABBA DOO
FIGGER IM BIGGER AND BETTER AND BAD-
    DER AND BABY LETS FACE IT
BOOM BAPPA
BLAKKA BLAKKA

PARAPA RAPA
BARAKA SHAKA
WAKA FLOCKA
OOOH MAMA MAMA
BABY BOWOWOW YIPPIE YO YIPPIE YAY BOW
WOW YIPPIE YO YIPPIE YAY
The engineer cut me off
"Could u go in again? The mic was off"
NO DOUBT
JAH RASTA
ALLAH ALLAH
YEMAYA CHANGO
WOOP WOOP
THAS THE SOUNDA DA POLICE
BRRANGDANGDANG
WE NEED FREEDOM
HEY MACARENA
SWING LOW SWEET CHARIOT
GLORY GLORY
HALLELULAH
L'CHAIM
SUPREME ALLAH NUMERICAL
SWAG ECCLESIASTICAL
SWAG EMIRATES
STONED IMMACULATE
PEACE IS REALITY
READ EM AND WEEP
GO WARRIORS
GO RAIDERS
GO NINERS
GO A'S
GO GIANTS

GO LAKERS
GO BULLS
GO DOLPHINS
GO CUBS
GO SOX
GO METS
GO PANTHERS
ALLAH
OM
OUR POWERS COMBINE
JAH ALLAH JAH ALLAH
AJUA
CAMPOS
OBATALA ACHE ACHE OBATALA AYE
OSHUN OSUN OLORUN AYE
CHANGO
SWOOP LACKADASICAL
GALLOP MAGNANIMOUS
WHATS A KING TO A GOD
WHATS A GOD TO A NON BELIEVER
HERE WE GO NOW
HEAR ME FLOW NOW
ALLAH
ALLAH

I laid many tracks that night, more than I could count on my two hands probably. They were all beautiful, perfect, immortal, immaculate, perpetual, incandescent, prismatic, but yeah most importantly, like I said, incandescent.

Came home, shook my wife's hand, made luh, felt good.

Baby was sleeping in the other room. Old think she grown ass…

17.

Mali and his girl Violin flew in from Brooklyn.

We went to this spot Jenny's, had brunch it was lit, it was my beautiful wife Khadija X, our girl Fatima X, me (MUHAMMAD X), Mali, Violin, Marty, Malika, Ali Ala, Munda.

That was a heady lil team, all hitters, so the day progressed thusly.

I like Mali and Violin cause they like to drink and shoot off they mouths. We was having some Haitian breakfast drink that involved rum, had a long esoteric history, tasted good. I think it was called "Aksan With Rum In It."

We talked about our Indian Man friend's screenplay about a Dominican Woman. Our thoughts were neutral to negative. We liked dude tho so we changed the subject: an old 2Pac song that was on where he raps about the Black Panthers for like ten minutes.

It was an impressive distraction from the present reality, truly artful, beautiful.

It was hella huevos, but a ham free event that time, Allah was in the building. No pork on our forks. We didn't dine on swine, and so forth.

I had a turkey leg, a grilled trout, a bite of grilled catfish, two poached eggs, a filet mignon, some grits, a coffee, a tea, a mimosa, a bloody mary, more of the Haitian stuff (conyo i think we took tequila shots too, they was all over the map), a little corncake with the molasses on it, a piece of fried chicken, a slice of watermelon, grapes, prosecco, kiwi, mango, papaya, pineapple, guava, coconut water straight out the young coconut,, that's what i got, i didn't care what anybody else got.

We all sat around and talked about sex, drugs, art, music, books, pornography, capitalism and its alternatives, crime, violence, race, class, culture, celebrity, obscurity, anonymity, the politics of the day-to-day, apathy, the guilt of "first world" privilege, globalism, the Internet, being broke, being poor, being rich, being in the middle, the "middle class," class, aspiration, myth, the prison industrial complex, spirituality, detachment, wonder, awe, spectacle, modernity, post modernity, theft, ownership, nature, the sun, the moon, the trees, the mountains, the oceans, the cosmos, mythical gods and real ones, life, death, love, wealth, poverty, racism, just a few things that were running thru our heads. There was some discussion about police brutality, socialism, sexism, Das Kapital, surfing, hacking, post modern architecture, 3D movies, the fourth, fifth, sixth, seventh and eighth dimensions. The ninth dimension. The tenth dimension. All the dimensions after that. There is a heaving bosom beneath the veil of language. There's a clumsy grace somewhere, whether within language or without it.

We rolled back to the crib in Paradise Hills put on some Cosmic Music. Some Peyote Chants. Free Jazz. Cecil Taylor. Creedence Clearwater Revival. Monk. Selda. Bird, Miles, Jones. Uh… Sun Ra, uh… Chicago Art Ensemble, Pharaoh Sanders, Anthony Braxton, Bob Marley, Cosmic Music again. Etc.

18.

Khadija and Fatima were rewatching The Labyrinth, I was reading some Borges in my left hand and Kiss of the Spider-woman in my right hand, Jorgito in the left eye and Puig in th' rite, all while Philly Joe from a couple chapters back solo'ed in the background.

Ravens circled overhead, maybe 12 of them, maybe 13. Hell maybe 23, I was drunk and not keeping score.

Ali Ala and Munda walked in from opposite sides of the room at the same time like two angels flanking the ill fresco.

"Hey MUHAMMAD X"

"Yo"

"Waddayoothinka Gravitational Time Distortion?"

"I Believe The Answer Is Within You."

"Taking another page from MULLAH X"

"Naw, a page from The Teachings. MULLAH X is just a Vessel of the The Teachings."

The conversation, as literally always, was wild Biblical in proportion. Numerous psyches were present.

"I feel sucked into the machine, producing pseudospiritual psychobabble por nadie y nada, furl meh," I told Ali Ala.

I told Ali Ala.

He said "Well for money"

I said "Like I said."

Conversation is the lowest form of telepathy. I fuck with conversation heavy.

The conversation skated around and came to a halt when Munda said: "The flower, the real flower, that's the best and most beautiful art, any other questions?"

My bride Khadija X, beautiful, turned, beautiful, to me and said: "What do u REALLY think of Gravitational Time Distortion?"

"Gravitational Time Distortion would be a crazy safe word."

That got some laughs.

We were already close to the end of a brief 18th chapter, kinda waiting it out til the 19th chapter.

I picked up my phone for the first time in hella long and tweeted at Capone and Nore something to the effect of "what's good."

No response.

Don't know why the idea sprang to mind. Probably something to do with Gravitational Time Distortion.

Fatima looked up from the Labyrinth, "Who's Albert Einstein?"

"No importa."

"It doesn't matter, joonie."

Fatima looked suspicious for a second then got up and poured a cup of tea, sipped it, looking out the window. The record stopped and she went to switch records. She picked Black Sabbath, Technical Ecstasy, threw that on and drank her tea, flipping thru the newspaper. Strange kid.

19.

We went to see Maya la Bruja. Fatima had eaten a magic mushroom, we wanted to know if it would kill her. I figured it wouldn't but we had to consult. She kept calling Fatima Black Cherry.

"BLACK CHERRY!"

She touched Fatima's forehead with two fingertips. Fatima seemed O.K., not freaked out, it seemed like a mellow trip.

"She threw up?"

"Yeah."

Maya fed her a drop of ink-black charcoal-based solution, a touch of molasses, a shot of lemon juice, a red seedless grape and a pomegranate seed, the whole while she was getting wafted with palo santo and sage and sandalwood and anointed with olive oil, coconut oil and rose water naked in a big gold bowl of water, real gold, real water.

All the water in the bruja's temple was purified by crystal pyramid (and reverse osmosis). It was real in every aspect.

We kicked it there for 7 hours. Checked my roly, it was midnite. The baby was totally fine, in high spirits, I read Treasure Island to her til she fell asleep. She woke up at dawn, I was dozing on a couch and she walked up, smacked the side of my head, "Wake up."

"I am up, poo butt."

"Let's blow this popsicle stand."

"Hold up."

I woke up her mom. Bruja Maya poured us some tea, I threw mine back, Khadija and Fatima left theirs.

"Peace no'bemo pronto."

"Si, paz, nos vemos muy pronto."

20.

At the crib with Khadija, Malika, Shadeh (she was pregnant too with the homie Ahmed's baby, he was on tour, a famed trumpeter), and Ali Ala. Marty was out somewhere. Some #blacklivesmatter folks had shut down the 405 in LA and wrote on the walls of the freeway all the names of all the unarmed men women and children, that the cops had killed without repercussion recently.

We were listening to Aragon and when that was done, Shadeh put on some Sade.

"What are u naming ur boy?" Malika asked Shadeh.

"Secret."

"Whoa, tight."

Khadija had made a mix of Persian and Thai Tea and Ali Ala had mixed some nice dark rum in with it for me and him, I added a splash of egg nog and a drop of maple syrup in mine, called it a Thai Prussian. Thought of a commercial for the Thai Prussian: Festive, pagan, global, Thai Prussian.

"Hey Ali Ala, I got a million dollar idea for u, the Thai Prussian."

"What, this drink?"

"Yeah."

"Good idea."

Fatima was lying on a $24,000 Persian rug reading Orhan Pamuk in Turkish.

"Which one is that?" I asked her. It came in a collection, they all had the same style cover.

"The White Castle."

"Any good?"

"O.K. so far."

The record ended and we put it on again.

Khadija ordered pizza, a rare occasion.

When the pizza mane came he was a Sikh brutha with the turban and the beard, he was like "My brother are u Sikh?" Pointing to my beard and the turban I forgot I had on at the time, I think Khadija had put it on me earlier that night. "Naw, I'm Cuban," I told him. He laughed and I didn't have the heart to tell him I wasn't joking. "Come upstairs, have a slice of pizza, I got some Pyramid Power Infused bottled water I'd like to sell u on," I told him. I had bought into a corner of Maya La Bruja's bottled water pyramid scheme. I had already bought into that Great Big Pyramid Scheme In The Sky, and once u buy into one Pyramid Scheme u buy into them all.

Upstairs I ran down the knowledge:

"See that pizza slice ur holding right there, that is a pyramid and it contains hella sacred powers..."

And so on.

He walked away with a bottle of Prismatic Crystal Pyramid water, a case to be delivered to his vacation home the next day and we had arrangements to receive 2.5 million in a Swiss account later that night.

"Two Thai Prussians, two million dollars."

"It was a good idea."

The money went thru later that night as planned. I arranged with my accountant to send Ali Ala some money for a flower arrangement delivery service he had recently started.

We threw on Swirling Dervish jams and got busy on some Thai Prussians, the conversation was philosophical in nature.

"Money is debt."

"Money is nothing."

"Money is absence."

"Money is death."
"Death is nothing."
Nobody was sure who was saying what, we were basically saying it all in unison.
Threw on Something Else by Cannonball Adderly, Fatima kissed me and Khadija each on the forehead and went to bed.
The convo continued:
"Jazzz."
"Like, wow, man."
"Wow daddio."
"Far out, groovy."
"Wowee Zowee."
"Swag Allah."
And so forth. The nite rolled into the inevitable morning.

21.

"U like that?"
"Yeah these ribs are smackin Sandy, they go super duper hard."
"Yup these ribs is hella maney."
"Ribs is crack."
"Ribs is fiy ma."
"These ribs are delicious."
"Quite tasty."

We were Sandy's house out in West Oakland, she had a big backyard with big ass tree in the middle. She had made some bomb ribs.

It was me, Khadija, Fatima, Riffs, his girl with the face tat, and then Sandy of course, and her roommates, Mendez (famous singer/songwriter), Emilio, Sammy, Slick, and JuJu (all of them in various bands, all of them at various points in time players in the rhythm section for Mendez, whom had seen a great deal of success and whom they all looked up to, me too, he was a good songwriter), plus Lena (who had just published a nonfiction book about some white boxers she had kicked it with in Duluth, Minnesota) was over with her dude Mark, guitarist in a pretty well known band too.

Mendez was a super gay black dude from the south, he was always hella loud at the party, I'm always thankful for fools who can be loud at the party cause being loud at the party is tiring and I prefer to kick back and watch and listen at a party. Lena was good at matching loud energy too so it was a nice lil roaring bonfire of a conversation. Plus there was a literal roaring bonfire going too.

Riffs had a love/hate relationship with Mendez and with Sandy too so he was something of a guest of honor and the atmosphere was a roast on the open fire of sorts. Plus there was a literal roast on the open fire.

But the real star of the night was Sandy's ribs.

At some point, I don't remember quite when or how, I was drunk off beer and whiskey and stoned too, the Riffs Roast seemed to turn into more of an argument and then close to what might have even been a fight and as if on cue Sammy, Slick and JuJu went in the garage and started playing that Doors song "This is the End."

Everybody walked down over to the garage and watched them play an entire set of Doors covers. They played them flawlessly, with total conviction. The Doors are a great band, some Alameda boys. Very good musicians, very good lyrics but an ultimately dumb band. Which isn't even an insult. I think it's a compliment actually. The Doors are a great, dumb band.

Anyway it was lit, we got fucked, wasted, blotto.

Khadija drove home while I slept it off. She ran a red on Masonic and a puerco materialized and pulled us over. He drew his pistol but Khadija was quicker and popped a few caps in his sorry ass, skirted on off, made it to the crib before the sirens and choppers started going.

We saw it on TV that night, Fatima was asleep, she had slept thru the cap popping too, or maybe just pretended to for deniable plausibility.

We decided not to tell Malika and Marty, Malika was too much of an alarmist, plus it seemed like it would blow over, enshallah. We considered another Hawaiian vacay but that mighta draw more suspicion so we stayed put and miraculously as if by the magic powers of Allah, it did blow over. Mashallah, Allah Hu Akbar, etc.

22.

Seven dove-white seagulls swooped from the sky and lifted the entire pizza up off the table we were seated at in the legendary Vittorio's Seaside Pizzeria in Sunset City. Fatima stood up clapping, a tear of joy rolling down her cheek.

She pointed at the sky and said: "LOVE."

The seagulls flew in seven different directions, each with their own slice of pizza.

Very auspicious.

Vittorio gave us a brand new pizza pie on the house.

Very auspicious indeed.

Malika and Marty had just moved into their own house out here, right across the street from the beach so Marty could surf everyday.

"We're way happier here than in Paradise Hills," Malika said.

"Makes sense," I said.

It was nice out in Sunset City.

"Maybe we should move here," I told Khadija.

"I like that place out in Mexico better," she said.

"Oh yeah."

I had forgotten all about that place.

"When do u want to move out there?"

"In 88 days."

"O.K."

I started the mental calendar.

Marty had spent his summers with his extended family close to Santa Sirena as a kid and talked about how beautiful it was at length.

"I heard Mexico is the land of mystery," I told him.

"Pues, sí."

The music was tight, surfy lil rock band.

"Who is this?" Khadija asked the busboy.

"Huh?"

"The music."

"Oh, hold on." He walked over to the bartender lady and asked her, came back, "Sunny and the Sunsets."

"No doubt, no doubt."

We walked past the zoo.

"U wana go to the zoo?" I asked Fatima.

"I don't want to support the enslavement of animals," Khadija said.

"Oh yeah," she was vegan, I always forgot. Fatima was vegan too tho she made gestural exceptions for symbolic reasons.

We posted up on the beach, watching the waves and whatnot. Marty passed me a flask and I took a swig of Bulleit.

It was a beautiful day in Sunset City. The sun set. It was a beautiful sunset in Sunset City.

23.

"Women be shopping."

"That's true, women do shop."

I was at this bar called El Mercado with Riffs talking shit.

"Fuck the police man."

"All cops are bastards."
"Remember school? That shit sucked."
"Barely went to that shit."
I had known Riffs since we were kids. Whenever conversation got slow, I'd ask about bit players of yesteryear and their whereabouts.
"How's Ricky?"
"That drunken loser?"
"How's Blunty Bill?"
"Moved to Vegas."
"How's Cee Cee?"
"Dead."
"Dang."
We were waiting on Big Maf, he was always in and out of town and today apparently he was in town and he owed Riffs some tiny amount of money so Riffs and me took it as an excuse to go drink beers and whiskeys at El Mercado while waiting for the big homie.
He was an hour late as usual, ordered a Hennessy.
"No Henny,"
Maf looked at me as if to say "what kind of establishment—" and I shrugged as if to say "I don't know."
"O.K. one whiskey but that's it. A nice one."
"What do u mean, a nice one?"
"Bruh."
We chit-chatted, bounced, hopped in the Bronco, burned a nice little hashy oowop while whippin over to a nearby Dim Sum spot in Chinatown, got some dim sum and drank Tsing Taos and tea.
My fortune cookie read:
"It's lit nigga turn up."
Riffs' read:

"Up the Punx! Oi! Oi! Oi!"

Maf's read:

"Smoke weed everyday."

All accurate fortunes.

Maf dropped us at my car and I gave Riffs a ride home, his main car had been seized and is other car was dead.

After I dropped off Riffs, I meandered thru the skreets listening to the latest E40 tape, it slapped.

The moon was out, I looked at the dark clouds.

It was a clear black night, a clear white moon.

Etc.

Made it to Paradise Hills, copped an ice tea and a Scratcher at the sev elev, won 100 bux. Copped another ice tea plus some grapes for Fatima and fizzy water for Khadija.

I got home and Fatima was asleep.

Khadija and me kissed around, watched a Marx Brothers movie, forget which one.

Threw on some Cecil Taylor, Khadija wasn't vibing on it, threw on some Art Blakey. Apparently that was more like it.

We drank some tea, smoked a doobie, she freestyled on the topic of Quantum Physics, Sufism, Black Holes, Hoodoo, various other matters of the heart, soul and head.

Khadija, beautiful peach, angel of the highest order, apple of mine eye, singer of soft songs and whatnot. KHADIJA X! QUEEN OF MYSTERY!

24.

It was 5:55 in the morning, I was in a black Lincoln Towncar sliding from Bushwick to BedStuy after a late session. We were in New York for a couple days for some sessions, interviews, etc., staying at Khadija's old apartment in the attic of a Catholic Church. The cab driver had on La Mega and it was Aventura on there. We have the same music publisher, Aventura and me, the whole publishing company eats off the royalties of that catalogue alone. Aventura man, that's some beautiful music.

When I got back, the baby was asleep in a big pile of blankets and Khadija was in deep meditation. The apartment was filled with candles and various idols and sculptures and religious imagery.

I rolled a lil fronto blunt and steamed dat, strolled around the block, bought a fried chicken leg and a can of coke, ate and drank them respectively on the walk back. Came back inside took a long shower. By the time I was done, Khadija was lying naked in bed so I joined her.

I laid down and listened to her channel Lord Krishna:

"I AM LORD KRISHNA, ALLAH HU AKBAR, JAH RASTA FARI, CHANGO, SEMA ANA EE. ENA ANA EKANDA. TRANQUILITY IS DIFFERENT FROM SATISFACTION. THE BLACK BUCK (VEHICLE OF CHANDRAMA, MOON) IS DIFFERENT FROM NOTHINGNESS/SUSPENDED ACTIVITY. EZIKIEL SAW THE WHEEL WITHIN THE WHEEL, ALLAH, ALLAH..."

I woke up, it was noon. I must have passed out at some point listening to the Krishna transmission, must have thrown me into a deep yogic sleep state. I must have needed that. Nusrat Fateh Ali Khan was singing that song that go like "Musta Musta." Certified slapper.

Khadija handed ur boy a cup of Persian tea. Wild pleasant.

"You fell asleep with a massive hard-on, I hope you don't mind I got on you and came on it."

"Oh word? Did I come too?"

"Yes, I'm pregnant again. Twins this time, fraternal, a girl and a boy."

"Damn, O.K., where's Fatima?"

"My cousin picked her up this morning took her to the Botanical Garden, we're going over to her and Jermaine's spot for dinner."

"Word O.K."

Roxana and Jermaine were sharp, well-read, well-dressed, traveled a lot. Jermaine collected masks and Roxana collected crystals. Their new crib was slightly bigger than their old crib, higher ceilings, bigger windows, walls lined with masks, shelves lined with crystals.

They fixed Dark & Stormies, Khadija, carrying twins, abstained.

After a few Dark and Stormies, we got it in our heads to take a cab to the Empire State building and have a look-and-see around the city from the bird's-eye-view, get the lay of the land if you will. Before we left, I raided their bathroom cabinet and found some vikes, popped a couple of those.

The city was lit. The view was legit.

Fatima said: "Wow! Far out! Groovy!"

"Glad u dig it mami."

Hella lights. Wild official. Sweet Pinball Stonehenge Nativity Scene. Golgotha. Moloch, the black smoke, the obelisks, the columns. We all kept singing "All of the Lights" humming the synthesized trumpet riff mostly.

There was a banker with a drunken party girl there, she was talking loud in a Russian accent, stopping only to sloppily make out with dude. It looked, oddly enough, like true love.

We shared a cab back to Brooklyn, the cab driver was the same Sikh dude who had delivered our pizza and bought into that Crystal Pyramid bottled water scheme.

"Wow, crazy coincidence man, how did that investment go."

"It broke me."

"Wow, sorry to hear that."

I made mental note to hit up Ali Ala, ask how that whole affair was doing, I had kind of handed off the reigns to him.

"So now you have to drive this cab for money."

"No, I do it for fun. I was born rich. Oil money. I have a lot of family in Saudi Arabia."

"Thought you were Indian."

"I am."

"Would you call yourself the black sheep of the family?"

"Why would u say that?"

"i don't know the question just popped into my head."

"It's an eccentric family."

He dropped us all back at Roxana and Jermaine's crib.

Fatima fell asleep on some blankets and we played dominoes, listened to Eddie Gale, drank red wine and smoked doobies (Khadija abstained). We ended up staying over, sleeping in their spare room.

We all woke up pretty early and got brunch at a nearby white people diner.

I ordered a steak and eggs and the bottomless mimosa.

After brunch we parted ways and we took Fatima to the Metropolitan Museum of Art.

She loved it.

New York is a hellof a town mane. I Love New York. I Heart New York.

New York, New York, feel me?

The City That Never Sleeps, The Big Apple, The Windy City.

Great pizza in New York.

We hung out there for a couple more days, rolling around, acting foolish, a couple meetings, sessions, interviews, but mostly doing nothing really, just living and feeling good. New York mane, wavy city, very groovy. Sweet town.

25.

"Zup."

"Churlin."

"Thazwazurp."

"Ayo!"

"Big Bwoy!"

"Ayyy!"

"Sup player."

"Sup peeyimpin."

"Where's Herman?"

"Fuck Herman."

"Herman sucks."

"Where's Magic?"
"Brazil."
"Oh tight."
We were in Hi-Five's backyard it was Hi-Five, Arkady, Mali, Elvin and Deedee.
"What's crackin."
'Same ol"
"Then why we here"
"U oughta kno"
"Hear ye!"
"Allah!"
"Order, order!"
The stenographer, Juanita, dutifully rattled all the crucial minutiae into orderly ink patterns on paper via outdated government issued machinery.
"High, bruh?"
"High mane."
"Kick me half that bag for old times"
"Fsho, there's bundles to go around."
"Ay what is this band?"
"The New Beautiful Sparkles"
"Ay where's White Dog and White Cat?"
"Iono"
Knowledge was dispersed. A sparkling black nite ensued. It was an hour when the devils was sleeping, we galloped around town like wild horses, stopping at watering holes and what have u.
Ended up at the Tremelo, owned by somebody expensive and important. The drinks were flowing for free. For whatever reason, the combination of souls in the room made all the liquor free. That was a nice feat to kick ur legs up to.

Khadija X landed her Persian carpet on the scene like "Where u been?"

"Around. I'm here now, how u? Where u been?"

I got her grapefruit juice and a Greyhound for myself, we found a booth.

"Good day?"

"O.K. day."

She sulked for a second and then weirdly, almost instantly, cheered up like she had just remembered something.

"There's a jukebox here, give me all ur quarters."

I had four exactly, think it came out to like 10 songs. Old jukebox, I think. She picked Michael Jackson: Human Nature and I picked out the rest:

Thin Lizzy: Jailbreak

Otis Redding: These Arms of Mine

Aretha Franklin: Do Right Woman

Bob Marley: Kinky Reggae

The Specials: Gangsters

The Clash: Lost in the Supermarket

Pulp: Common People

Smiths: This Charming Man

Ray Charles: Georgia

A weird line-up, I was just kinda surfing the juke box. It definitely was an old jukebox.

Jermaine and Roxana slid thru we kicked it with them for a while, ate some fried potatoes, I had another beer, I started feeling sleepy.

MULLAH X came in like: "KUJICHAGULIA!"

I woke right up, he looked around saw a decent crowd and went:

"PEACE TO THE SOULS AND FAMILIES OF QUINTONIO LEGRIER AND BETTIE JONES! PEACE TO

THE SOULS OF ALTON STERLING AND PHILANDO CASTILE! PEACE 2 THE SOUL OF FREDDIE GRAE! ERIC GARNER! MICHAEL BROWN! TRAYVON MARTIN! OSCAR GRANT! AMADU DIALLO! SEAN BELL! ABANDON DEATH CONSCIOUSNESS! DEATH IS NOTHING! LOVE IS EVERYTHING! LOVE IS ALL AROUND U! WE R ALL PERFECT, WE WILL ALL DIE & RECOMBINE IN 2 EVERYTHING OVER & OVER 4EVR. FEAR WILL DIE. THERE IS A FEELING BEHIND THE IMMEDIATELY PERCEIVED REALITY THAT CAN BE APPREHENDED IN A DARK AND QUIET STILLNESS. KEEP TRYING TIL U DIE OR ALSO MAYBE U WON'T EVEN DIE CONSIDER THAT OPTION. A LOT OF ASPECTS OF THIS REALITY ARE WACK AND WILL FIND THEMSELVES EXTINCT. DEATH IS A CONCEPT THAT MASKS, REVOLVES, PUNCTUATES, BUT ONE THING IT CAN'T DO IS LIVE. ALL LIFE IS ETERNAL, ALL EXISTENCE IS INFINITE, DEATH IS NOTHING. SWAG INFINITY SWAG IMMACULATE OUR HEARTS ARE A THOUSAND DIAMONDS MY SPIRITUAL POETICS ARE UNDENIABLE. CARVE A CAVE IN THE AIR WHERE UR THOTS CAN LIVE. YA TU. ENDLESS FUNK SADLY SPRINGS FORTH FROM ENDLESS PIMPIN YET BEHOLD THAT SAME PIMPIN HAS PEOPLED THE EARTH, IS THE NATURE OF MAN 2 SIN DOE? NAY! RELIGION IS OFT ADMINISTERED IN A COWARDLY FUNCTION BUT THE CONCEPT OF GOD DROPS LIKE A GENTLE STRAIN O HONEY 2 TH' BRAIN. U ONLY TALK ABOUT "GOD" WHEN U NEED "GOD" THAT'S HOW LANGUAGE WORKS. BETTER THAN TALKING IS THINKING, AY DIOS

MIO ALLAH CHANGO ALLAH JAH RASTA SWAG STUPENDOUS, STONED IMMACULATE, SWAG PERPENDICULAR, THE PLASMATIC AND PRISMATIC CONVERGE, WOW. BUT YAL DON'T HEAR ME THO. BUT MORE IMPORTANTLY PEACE TO THE SOULS AND FAMILIES OF TAMIR RICE, SANDRA BLAND, MIKE BROWN, ERIC GARNER, OSCAR GRANT, TRAYVON MARTIN, SEAN BELL, AMADOU DIALLO Y TODO ALLAH CHANGO JAH RASTAFARI ALLAH ALLAH."

"ALLAH."

26.

"See the pretty bodies fly," said Arkady as we walked across el puente to Manhattan, "closer to the ground am I."

I said: "No doubt."

Hi-Five rolled up on us on a bike.

"Zup."

"Peace Allah."

"I got some drogas, u want to sniff them at The Partridge, have some drinks?"

"Sounds good."

We stopped into The Partridge, got gin and tonics, took turns going into the luxurious washroom to speedball and then sat sipping the g & t's looking out the front window, soaking up the sun rays, it was beautiful out.

Khadija X putted up on a Harley. I ordered her a grapefruit juice.

She had just come up from Washington D.C. where she had led a meditation at the Turkish Embassy.

Roxana and Jermaine were watching Fatima in Brooklyn.

White Bird and El Cid trotted up on horses. White Bird's horse was black, El Cid's horse was white. White Bird tipped his hat at us all and galloped off, El Cid dismounted his steed and harbored him on a parking meter. We ordered another round of g & t's. Khadija, with child again, abstained.

The conversation was like:

"Ay"

"Sup"

"Ay"

"Sup"

and so forth.

"Truth, Beauty, Justice, Faith, Intelligence, Agency, Genius, Wizardry, Lost Innocence, Extralinguistic Desire, Perpetuity, Words carved in rock, versus stained on paper, versus lite, electric, crystal, the nothing between the atoms, dark matter, mystery, peace."

Chapter 26 ended abruptly.

27.

"So what."

"Who cares."

Me and Khadija and Fatima were back in Paradise Hills, Khadija was popping popcorn, I was rolling around on the $24k Persian rug with Fatima, Bo Diddley was playing on the record player.

We had been having some sort of boring argument that neither of us were invested in having and so decided to stop arguing and enjoy the incredibly beautiful mellow sunset.

We watched Casa Blanca and ate popcorn. It was dark now and it started to rain.

We put Fatima to sleep.

Chapter 27 ended hella abruptly too

28.

"I'm at the hood party."

"What?"

"The hood party."

The phone cut off.

I was at the hood party.

And apparently whoever that was that had called me was at the hood party too. The world is a ghetto.

I was drinking some pink champagne in South Paradise Hills at Khadija's girl Babs' house feeling regal. Khadija X had come into the possession of a projector and was projecting a skate video my dude Addie had made. Maf, Riffs and the Dangler were over. Babs' dude Darius was out somewhere.

We smoked some hookah and drank tea. Some smoked some hash and then some opium.

The skate video ended and we put on M.A.S.H. and listened to some Ace Hood mixtape.

Malika, Marty and Ali Ala came over.

Malika and Ali discussed some legal issues, some political issues, both personal and global, like, I would say, everything.

Afrooz and the homie Keita swam thru. Mali and Violin rolled in. It was a lot of cognac and tree after that, then we dabbed some shatter, I didn't appreciate the rigmarole involved with dabbing shatter but enjoyed the highs and conversations.

More tea and hookah. Somebody put on a Velvet Underground record. Some weed cookies were passed around.

Hi Five was in town with Jorgito, Carlito and Lito, they slid thru with lean. Medina and Roxana showed up. Munda, Sueña and Maya La Bruja showed up. Mullah X showed up, proclamated: "ALLAH…" etc. We sat rapt, hearts ablaze, concepts of god trickled down 'pon uz like gentle strains o' honey from heaven and radiated into our beings. We were all radios.

29.

I was back in The Hague again, in the penthouse suite of the Hotel Des Indes, looking over the city smoking a hash spliff listening to Meek Mill's Dreamchasers 2 or maybe Dreams and Nightmares 2 I forget which one. It sounded good. Meek Mill had bars and the production was flawless.

I had court the next morning but was free all night, wondering what to do next. I had just got off a lil video chat with the wife and kid, they were kicking it with Malika and Marty in Sunset City. I flipped on the TV.

A Busta Rhymes music video.

I ordered champagne, fell asleep, woke up to a knock, it was the champagne.

I drank the champagne and smoked another hash joint, flipped the channel.

A murder of crows, a murmuration of starlings...

Flipped the channel.

Scarface.

Watched that.

Went out hit a nice Chinese spot.

Dangler was in town too, he had a court date tomorrow too it turned out, I had forgotten that until just now, I had been traveling a lot, my mind was foggy. I hit him up.

We went to some bar had beers, he had been record shopping all day.

"Find anything?"

"Rare Hot Albacore record."

"Any good?"

"Decent, but it's worth a lot more than I paid for it."

"Where they from again?"

"The bay actually, South Sunset City, Rodeo Valley."

"U can't find the record out there?"

"U can but it's rare. They pressed it out here."

"Oh ha crazy."

I switched to whiskey, Dangler stuck with beers.

The bartender took a shot with ur boy.

We kicked it there then headed to some sort of gala the Dangler's Homie Marvelous had set up, some sort of red velvet on cobblestone old timey event, torches aflame down some hallway, real European shit.

Wandered into what looked to be a recording studio, spit a freestyle:

AYO MOONCHILD
SWEET SOUL CHARIOT
HIGH IN THE SKY LIKE THE SUN
SO ARROGANT
DIPPED IN PARABLE
SOUL SO WEARABLE
SEE HOW THEY SOLD
SO MANY BUT NONE OF THEM COMPARABLE
MANE SO MANY BUT NONE A DEM RESEMBLE HIM
AND HIM IS ME
KOOL A.D.
NUMBER ONE RAPPIN ASS RHYMING MC
A GOD WITH HIS EARTH AND HIS SEED I BE
AND THATS LOVE
I DON'T NEED I.D.
FLY LIKE DOVE
U CAN SEE MY PEACE
GET AROUND LIKE A WHEEL SO I NEED THAT GREASE

PEACE TO THE GODS IF I CAN BE THAT GREEK
I BE THAT AFRO INDO ASIASTIC SOUL SO ORIGINAL MAN
REAL NIGGA WASUP
GODDAMN
ALLAH HU AKBAR
RUNNIN FROM THE COP CAR
BOOM SHAKANARNAR
JAH RASTAFARI
CHANGO
CHANGO
BRUH IM JURASSIC PARK
IM THE CONGO
AVE LA SANTA MARIA COMO MONGO
SEE ME IN MIAMI IN A CONDO
BLOWIN THAT SKRONG THO
PAZ A CHICAGO
Y TODO MI PRIMOS Y MANOS
TATO
420 IN A 911
I GOT 7 FELONIES
FREE PALESTINE
PEACE ALLAH
JAH JAH
CHANGO
ALAMEDA COUNTY EAST BAY HO

30.

"Give me some room."

We had just had marital relations and were in a tangle.

I turned over, she turned over, we were both faced outward like gargoyles protecting a box of jewels.

Some minutes passed. Fatima yelped in the other room.

I went over and plucked her from her crib plopped her between us, the box of jewels, we all fell asleep.

We all dreamed the same dream.

A big open obsidian floor with alternating obsidian and ivory columns and no ceiling or walls on top of a green hill overlooking a sparkling blue ocean, big blue sky, some clouds here and there, purple mountains in the distance. This was our home apparently.

I put on a Ray Charles record and shot dice with myself while they wandered the orchards selecting the apples for our dinner.

At dinner we sat around a large golden bowl of water and drank with our hands, ate our apples. The water was sweet.

We walked down the hill to a wide river with a calm shaded swimming hole tucked in a hilly corner on the way to the ocean.

After bathing there we swam across to the strong current and floated out to the beach. Some turtles swam neath us, nudging our feet with their noble noses.

The water got hotter and bubblier and we realized we were swimming towards an underwater volcano. I swam inside while Khadija and Fatima waited for me.

In there was a Djin, I bought shell from him for a slightly smaller shell I had stored in a pouch of my all white (Gucci) swim trunks. And with this transaction I woke up.

My wife and child were still asleep next to me.

I walked into the kitchen had a glass of water.

Walked outside and looked at the moon. It was full.

I felt hyper real, earthly.

There were lights in the distance.

A lot of people on earth.

Even more stars in the sky, hard to see that in a city sometimes.

Joy is neither a privilege nor a right, it's an organic eventuality.

31.

I was at the Olympiatic Hotel in New Orleans, poolside with a mojito watching a Fellini movie being projected on the wall. I had a court date the following morning and was enjoying a day by the pool. I hit the hot tubs then the sauna then the steam room then jumped in the pool swam a couple laps and had another mojito, watched the movie, I did variations of this all day. A waiter sold me some OxyContin, hadn't popped one of those in a while, I was feeling hella wavy.

Eventually I retired to my room and read some of my book. I was rereading Crime and Punishment by the Russian homie Fyodr Doestoyevsky. I got bored and flipped on the TV, more Fellini, musta been a marathon.

Flipped the channel:

Family Guy

Flipped the channel:

Ghostbusters

Flipped the channel:

C-Span

Went back to the Fellini marathon.

Ordered some champagne to the room had another rocko, took a long shower when I came out the champagne was there in a nice bucket of ice. The hotel was old timey, expansive, well-wrought, prob used to be a big attraction.

I called up Khadija.

"My bride."

"My groom."

"How's the monkey?"

"Chillin."

"Where u at?"

"Malika's. When u back?"

"Late tomorrow with any luck."

"Come tonight."

"O.K."

I called the front desk had them charter me a private jet and call me a car, got dressed, headed down to the lobby, it was hella crowded. A fully decked out chauffeur, hat, gloves, everything, tapped me on my shoulder and led me to the black Lincoln out front. We rolled to the airport and I hopped on the PJ.

Was in Paradise Hills that night, Malika watched Fatima while me and Khadija caught a movie at the repertory theatre. Kirostami joint, Taste O' Cherry.

The next day we took Fatima on a hike in the woods, Khadija pulled a big thin cotton paisley blanket out her little straw bag and spread out a lil picnic us in a meadow, loaf of bread, bottle of water, bottle of wine for the two of us, three oranges. It was wild pleasant.

"What do u want to be when u grow up, Fatima?"

"Astronaut."

"Swag, swag."

32.

We were in the waiting room of The Future Primitive Art School, Fatima was applying to get in. Nice spot out on Cherub Hill in San Francisco, great view.

They called her name. We were led down a corridor to a large auditorium with a full length basketball court. An Afgani woman in a burqa threw Fatima a basketball and she sunk a cross court three, an olive skinned man in a sharp gray Ferragamo suit said, "Congratulations, ur in."

It was simple as that. She began classes immediately, was led to a room of 4 boys and 3 girls her age standing in a row. She got in line. An Iraqi woman in an Abaya said:

"LOVE IS A DREAM."

The kids all answered (Fatima too, she's quick):

"AND THE DREAM IS REAL."

The woman said:

"DO WHAT U LOVE."

And the kids answered:

"AND LOVE HOW U FEEL."

"Class dismissed."

We took Fatima over to a bookstore and had her run around and pick out a book. She found a nice hardcover "first edition" (whatever that means) Egyptian Book of the Dead.

We copped her that and sped home to Paradise Hills in the white Ferrari La Ferrari.

She sat on a hammock in the backyard reading and we lamped on some new outdoor furniture Khadija had recently come into the possession of on the deck that Marty had built when he was still living there.

Khadija said: "Let's move into that spot in Baja now."

"It hasn't been 88 days yet."

"It's been 88 years."

"Ur math is spiritual."

We loaded up the Black 2014 Jeep Wrangler with crystal, amethyst, bismuth, gold, some silver and some electrum and hit the winding 1, saw the Pacific snake alongside us for hours til we found ourselves at our Mexican beach house over Santa Sirena way.

The next few months we spent planting palms and banana trees, succulents, magnolia, jasmine, tomatoes, corn, Marijuana, mint, Rosemary, chamomile, sage, uña de gato, avocado, lemon, lime, orange, tobacco, African daisies.

We were a five minute walk down the hill to the beach so we swam and sunbathed every day. We walked around the cliffs, came back made little meals. I caught up on some reading, Bolaño, Murakami, Fante, Bukowski, Angela Davis, Zinn, Hawking, Malcolm X, Richard Wright, Baldwin, Tanehisi Coates, Mira Gonzalez, Tao Lin, Spencer Madsen,

Sandra Cisneros, Alex Chee, Porochista Khakpour, Anne Carson, Toni Morrison, bell hooks, Eldridge Cleaver, Hemingway, Burroughs, Hermann Hesse, Marquez, Junot Diaz, Danzy Senna, Zadie Smith, Borges, Breece D'j Pancake, DFW, Raymond Carver, Gordon Lish, Atticus Lish, Flannery O'Connor, Zorah Neale Hurston, Jean Toomer, Ralph Ellison, Aime Cesaire, Jamaica Kincaid, Edwidge Danticat, the Bible, the Koran, the Tao Te Ching, the Bagavad Gita, Rumi, Hafez, Lorca, Marti, Bob Kaufman, Chinua Achebe, etc.

Then a long period with no reading.

I don't know how long we stayed there. Felt like two perfect days.

33.

We we were at the beginning of the second act, living in Mexico, Fatima commuting via helicopter to The Future Primitive Art School in San Francisco where she was majoring in Astronautics, me and Khadija tending to the garden, beach bumming, occasionally overseeing large exports from the ports.

Fatima began building her own rocket ship in the hills out past the house. She had a little corrugated tin club house equipped with all the finest Astronautical equipment she could carry by helicopter home from school. I didn't ask her if she had obtained these materials with permission, I assumed she knew what she was doing.

She had two friends, Rosa and Guadalupe, they were twin sisters. Their mother Maria sold beautiful woven rugs and painted clay pots in a stall on the tourist strip. We had bought some when we first came thru and the kids got along. Sometimes Maria, Rosa and Guadalupe would come over for dinner. Maria didn't know any English but she could put down some tequila so we got along. An old mistico would come around too, his name was Maestro Hakim Karim Karim Hakim Allah (Hakim or Karim or Karim Hakim or Hakim Karim or Maestro Hakim or Maestro Karim or Maestro Hakim Karim or Maestro Karim Hakim for short). He was from Clink Town up norte, not far from where I spent much of my youth. He lived in Santa Sirena now, down the way from us in a one room adobe house and sometimes he came thru to drink tequila with me and Maria on the front deck overlooking the ocean. Khadija would kick it but she didn't like tequila mostly stuck to tea. Maestro Karim Hakim would bring his guitar and play songs, mostly in English but some in Spanish. Over time he came to be in a romantic relationship with Maria and she'd sometimes stay over there with her kids.

Usually when we were all kicking it, the kids were off building that outer space rocket ship of Fatima's design. There were only three seats on the rocket ship. We all understood they had not included any of us in their interstellar travel plans.

I had looked over the blueprints they were fantastic, it looked like the puppy would fly. The days passed and the rocket really began to shape up.

One sunny day, we were on the deck with Maria and Hakim when Fatima came running up to the house, Rosa and Lupe trailing after her.

"It's done, me and Lupe and Rosa are going for a test drive, come watch the launch."

We did. It was spectacular. The thing shot up like a rocket.

Very fast, very high in the air. We were all a bit nervous but it obviously was a very well built rocket. It kept climbing higher until it disappeared into the sky. We waited but it didn't return.

I remembered the radio receiver Fatima had built for us back at the house, we headed back over and flipped on telecommunications, received word that all was well, they were headed to Mars might not be back for a year or so. The lil devils! We drowned out sorrows in tequila and began waiting for our kids to come back.

Time passed. It was a capable squad, I had full confidence they would do alright I just missed Fatima was all. But of course kids always go their own way.

34.

"It's all bullshit."

"Ya tu."

Riffs was visiting our Snta. Sirena crib from up north, was drunk and proclamatory.

It was him, Maestro Karim, Maria, Khadija and me drinking beers on the deck, ocean shushing in the dark beyond us, peaceful night.

"Eat and sleep and live and breathe and shit and fuck and fucking die, it's bullshit."

"U right, u right."

"It's bullshit."

"No doubt."

"Bullshit."

"No doubt."

Japanese psych band The Mops was on.

We switched to tequila.

We smoked a doob, put on the Isley Brothers.

Smoked another doob, put on Paul Butterfield Blues Band.

Smoked another doob, put on It's a Beautiful Day.

Smoked another doob, put on Bloodstone.

Riffs went and passed out in the guest room.

Karim and Maria went off to Karim's spot.

Me and Khadija sat looking at the waxing crescent moon and the Milky Way. Our little angel was up there in her homemade rocket with her two besties. We wondered when she'd make it home. Saw a couple shooting stars. Started getting cold and went in.

Riffs peeled out after breakfast, he was meeting up with some folks in Tijuana.

We went down and lamped on the beach.

I looked up in the sky and noticed something incoming. A little space capsule parachuting out of the clouds. It plunked into the water about a mile out. We swam out there. When we got the there, Fatima, Lupe and Rosa were posted up. They had laid some towels out on the bobbing capsule and were sunbathing with some bottles of Coke.

We climbed onto the capsule and hugged them. I kissed my lil Fatima on the forehead. I jumped into the cockpit of the capsule. The seat was comfy, I remember taking her to pick up the artisanal leather. This is where Fatima had been cooped up. Hard to believe she was into that lifestyle but kids will be kids.

We all swam back and I called up Maria, she came over with tears in her eyes and some mild rebukes en español but mostly joy, Maestro Hakim trailing behind her and rubbing her shoulders to calm her down.

We all had dinner together, salad from the garden and two roast chickens.

"How was Mars?"

"Beautiful."

She started talking about a bigger rocket to take us all. I was into it.

"I'm going to build us all a house on Mars," she said.

"I'm with that."

35.

"Anything."

I was early for court in San Francisco, had ducked into a white people bar downtown.

"What do u mean, anything?"

"Anchor Steam and a shot of Bulleit."

"Coming right up."

Older white dude in a brown mustache at the bar said, "Peruvian rice."

"Excuse me?"

"Invest in Peruvian rice, it's low right now and due for a boom."

"Isn't that how Emperor Norton lost it all?"

Emperor Norton was a famous rich San Francisco eccentric who had apparently lost it all on Peruvian rice, at least that's what I had heard.

"That was a long time ago, I'm telling u now's the time for Peruvian rice."

"Put me down for a hundred shares, then."

I was still up from my Crystal Pyramid Bottled Water venture and what can I say, ur boy like to gamble.

I called up Ali Ala and passed along the tip, he was a gambling man too.

After my second beer I realized I was late for court, cut out.

Court was O.K. The judge was an old white man with a long white beard, long white hair and a wizard hat, he said: "Islam is peace or nah?"

I said: "Islam is peace."

Judge said: "Peace is reality or nah?"

I said: "Peace is reality."

Where was my lawyer at? Shouldn't she be answering these questions? Well, no matter, I guess.

The judge said: "Endless pimping equals what?"

I said: "Endless funk."

The judge said: "What is truth?"

I said: "Paradox."

The judge said: "Ur free to go."

I went to pick up Fatima at over at the Future Primitive Art School and we rode the chopper back to our modest beach house in Santa Sirena.

Along the way, she showed me blueprints of her new rocket ship. It slept 20. She was thinking of a lil Mars commune. I was with that.

She read to me from her assigned book of dichos.

"Amor con amor se paga."

"Eso es la verdad, mami."

"Donde hay gana, hay maña."

"True, true."

"El que anda con lobos a aullar se enseña."

"¡Ay! ¡Ya lo sé!"

We came home and Khadija had on a Cannonball Adderly record, was making pasta. Fatima and I read out on the deck under the deck lamp and the vast sprawling milky guey. She read her dichos and I read The Mambo Kings Sing Songs of Love by Oscar Hijuelos, white Cuban dude out of New York, good writer, good book.

36.

"We built this city."

We were in a large stone ziggurat, location to remain undisclosed. We were all robed, hooded, masked, twelve of us in all. I had a pretty good idea who like 4 or 5 of the other folks there were and I could venture a guess on the remaining 7 or 8. We were drinking a delicious 100 year old Pinot Noir spiked with a mixture of blood drawn by sacramental dagger from the left palm of each person seated at the circular table. Twelve white doves circled above us in a counterclockwise swirl. Above them, twelve black crows circling clockwise. Above those, twelve white owls, counterclockwise, above those twelve black ravens, clockwise. Twelve torches flamed. A circular candelabra with twelve giant red candles hung above us. It was all a little much.

"Hate to be a drag yal but I gota dip mane this whole vibe is tripping me out, not really my scene."

They all pointed their black velvet gloved fingers at me. I bolted, ran down a dark torchlit hallway, ducking swinging axes and flurries of arrows, somehow made it out there alive.

Ended up at the old downtown San Francisco white people bar from the last chapter.

"U were just in here yesterday, 'nother court date?"

"Yeah."

"Bulleit and Anchor Steam?"

"Pinot Noir."

"Fancy."

Same mustachioed dude from last time with the Peruvian rice tip.

"How's Peruvian rice man, I haven't called up my accountant."

"Not so good."

"U fuckin bum."

"Soy un perdidor man, I'm a loser baby."

"Eh, buy u a beer, what's ur name soldier?"
"Muhammad X."
"Muslim brutha."
"Yep. U?"
"Agnostic."
The bartender slid him a beer, said to me: "That's Emperor Norton."
"THEE Emperor Norton?"
"The one and only," said the Emperor. He tipped his beer slightly, spilled some, barkeep wiped it with a towel immediately.
"I thought u were long dead."
"Hearsay."
"So u got fucked twice by Peruvian Rice?"
"It's been one long fuck but the nut is gona be sweet."
Ew.
"I'll trust u on that."
I let my hundred shares of Peruvian rice ride. I'm a gambling man and what had I to lose? Money is nothing.
Billie Holiday: In My Solitude came on. Beautiful number. We all sat and listened.
I finished my beer and went to go scoop Fatima from Future Primitive Art School, in the chopper ride home she read me some more dichos:
"El que temprano se moja, tiempo tiene de secarse."
"¡Conyo!"
"El que nada no se ahoga."
"Ay! Ay! Ay!"
Got home and Khadija had on a Francoise Hardy record, was baking some fish and and diced potatoes in an herby lil sauce for din din. Fatima worked on her blueprints in her room. She was outsourcing construction in Russia and China,

would have the rocket shipped in parts here and assembled by a crew of sturdy Mexicans she had vetted from the docks. She was becoming a real bossalini. I drank a couple Pacificos on the deck looking at the moon.

Abuse of power comes as no surprise. Absolute power corrupts absolutely. Is powerlessness innocence then? Nay, methinks. Morality is a theatre, good and evil are illusory, there are no pure or just ideological positions, all that exists is powers in relation to powers.

Those were some thoughts that passed thru my head but none of them sounded right. They all sounded faulty, if not completely out and out wrong.

How about: everything is, nothing isn't. Or how about nothing at all?

I felt like I was wandering thru a casino. Wait was I? I hit a lick and came up a few hunnit bills.

37.

A cab picked us up from the house and took us over to the airport, we were headed to Istanbul, Khadija had some family there and had chartered us a spacious flying carpet.

It was my first time traveling by flying carpet and it was less windy than I thought it would be, it was like comparable to like a convertible doing 70 on the highway. Pretty mellow, refreshing. The weather over the Atlantic was surprisingly warm. The sky was clear midnite blue and sparkling with stars. The waves below all sweet and wavy.

We had packed light, a samovar of Persian tea, 3 silver cups, and a plate of baklava all on a silver tea tray.

Fatima was juiced.

"Fuck rocket science," she said, "the flying carpet is the future."

She decided to sell her rocket blueprint and half-built rocket to a Chinese aeronautical firm to finance the purchase a couple hundred kilos of flying carpet thread and a state of the art weaving loom.

When we landed in Istanbul, Fatima made some calls and went thread and loom shopping. Me and Khadija hit a beautiful ancient bathhouse for a long scrub, soak and steam. Sun streamed into the main bathing room thru intricately carved stone ceiling tiles. Then we got some more baklava and some Turkish coffee. Then we hit the Ayasofya and the Blue Mosque, the little underground aqueduct thing with the giant stone Medusa head in it and the old royal palace turned museum. It was early in the morning so not very crowded anywhere.

We met up with Fatima in a nice Kebabery on the top floor of a 5 story building in a sort of hipster neighborhood across town from all the tourist shit, had some lunch and walked around that part of town, ended up at a plush, low lit hookah bar and smoked some shisha while listening to an old man shred solemnly on the oud. Khadija's uncle Kadir slid thru and we drank a licorice flavored liquor called Raki all night. Kadir was a banker, I asked him about Peruvian rice, he advised against it.

The next morning, we took a boat out to an island where Khadija's aunt Lale lived. Dolphins were leaping alongside the boat, a waiter came by and served us tea and we sipped, watching the dolphins.

We landed on the island. Tight little old timey spot, cobblestones, horse drawn carriages. We took a carriage up the hill to Lale's house. It was a two horse carriage, one white, one brown, both quite healthy.

We got there she had breakfast ready, a Turkish egg dish with peppers and onions called Menemen, delicious, some bread, some Feta cheese, honey, jams, Turkish coffee, baklava, tea, figs, all spread out on a big wood table in the backyard. Bruh, it was a delight.

I got up and tapped my glass with a spoon and was like:

"Many men, wish death upon me
Blood in my eye dog and I can't see
I'm trying to be what I'm destined to be
And niggas trying to take my life away
I put a hole in nigga for fucking with me
My back on the wall, now you gon' see
Better watch how you talk, when you talk about me
'Cause I'll come and take your life away
Many men, many, many, many, many men
Wish death 'pon me
Lord I don't cry no more
Don't look to the sky no more
Have mercy on me"

I received hearty applause.

We hit the beach for the rest of the day. Lale and her friend Kiraz and Kiraz's daughter Pembe all came with us.

Fatima and Pembe giggled around in the water and we laid out in the sun sucking beers and jumping in the water to cool off and then go lay down again and dry off. We stayed there til the light changed and headed back for dinner. Kebab, rice, bread, beer, wine, coffee, Raki. We slept over and spent the next two days there in almost identical fashion then hopped on a boat back to Istanbul.

Lale, Kiraz and Pembe came along with us. They went around the city all day with Khadija and Fatima and I drank Raki and beer all day with Kadir in the bar below his apartment. It started to feel like he owned the bar, like the bar was his house. It was tight, we were kicking it in dude's big ass house now. He was a serious drinker and I did my best to keep up.

A couple days later we were back in Santa Sirena, Fatima had set up her loom and was at work on her intergalactic flying carpet. Khadija had bought a loom of her own and was weaving a rug for the living room. I was lying on the couch still nursing my Raki hangover, listening to Erik Satie, drinking tea, nibbling a weed cookie.

I squinted out the window and spotted Marty and Malika's car coming up the dirt road to our house. Oh shit, I forgot they were coming today.

Khadija and Fatima showed Marty and Malika around the area while I took a nap then we had some tacos and Coronas over at Francisco's.

Came back watched the Simpsons, had Lapsang Souchong and a couple Indios.

Frank Zappa came on the TV it was rare.

Flipped the channel it was THE SUNSET PRAYER (Salatu l'Maghrib)

Consisting of 3 moments:

A. ALLAH HU AKBAR

B. AL-FATIHAH (QORAN, CH. 1)

C. SURAT AL-KAFIRUN (Qoran, Ch. 109)

RUKU, SUJUD, etc.,

SURATU L-IKLAS (Ch. 112)

Or at least that's what the text in the bottom left screen had read, I felt it at the time useful to memorize this tidbit of info. Call it a nervous tic.

Flipped the channel it was a witch, a tiger, a hobo, and a clown. For some reason, the Islamic Liturgy from the previous channel lingered here in this scene as background music.

It was quite the spectacle, we were all enthralled. Then matters turned to more serious concerns. We got fucked up on tequila, Maestro Hakim (Maestro Karim Hakim Allah was his full name, Karim or Hakim for short) and his Maria came thru. Fatima had Lupe and Rosa on embroidery they were doing truly divine work. The flying carpet would be done in 7 days.

Marty said he had to run stateside tomorrow to surf a lil contest and he'd be back the next day, hitting some spot south of here with Baby Moose and Weedy, I asked him to cop me some art stateside, two pieces by this San Diego Mexican graffiti writer GRASA they were rare abstract pieces.

We threw on some Last Poets. Then some Chicago Art Ensemble.

One day turned into another one again.

38.

This girl is rich.

And she fly she fly she fly.

That was the song that was playing.

We were in the Penthouse Suite of the Burj Al Arab.

Fatima was drawing up blueprints of intergalactic meta-Islamic, post Oriental flying carpets, I was listening to Sketches of Spain lying on a white leather couch. Khadija was in deep meditation. I guess I was too.

I suddenly realized I was paying an offering of psychic energy to my daughter without even having first noticed it. Me and wifey both. I sat up and curled my legs up like Khadija's, regulated my breathing and sharpened the focus of my psychic energies, clearing my head and transmitting swift, pure unmitigated love to my seed.

Her blueprints were exquisite, kaleidoscopic, each lil floral paisley tendril placed in runic harmony, she was a soulful engineer, the thing would fly, would most definitely reach the farthest corners of the cosmos. I could hardly believe she had once been a wee tadpole swimming in my nether bag. It was way past her bedtime but who cares, she was doing her thing.

Khadija and I meditated on thru the nite while Fatima dutifully wrought her flying carpet blueprints. When the sun rose over the sparkling Persian Gulf, Fatima went to bed and Khadija made some tea. We looked over the blueprints, nodding in approval and then gazed at the Dubai skyline bathed in blue pink dawn sunlight. Impressive stuff. We took a bath together and had some spiritual relations. We fell asleep in the big ass comfy bed.

Woke up to Fatima crawling into bed with us. She rolled around, snuggling and cooing and then started tugging at our ears and eyelids and noses and hair until we woke up. It was one in the afternoon.

We hit one of the hotel's many luxurious and expansive swimming pools for a dip and a sun bathe then Khadija and Fatima hit the mall, I stayed poolside for a while then headed back to the suite and slept some more.

Woke up to some grilled fish and Greek salad being delivered to the suite. Khadija and Fatima were on the couch surrounded by Gucci, Prada, Louis Vuitton and Fendi bags watching the 1928 Joan of Arc. Intense and beautiful movie. Renée Falconetti is a revelation.

We ate our dinner watching the tragically heroic zealotry of Yung Joan then we headed over to the helicopter pad and a large eagle came swooping down and grabbed us in its powerful talons and flew straight up into the sky, straight to the moon, dropping us in a beautiful cold barren white sand desert and taking back off flying off to some distant nebula.

"Remind me to look into the construction of Eagles," said Fatima, "I think that's my next venture after flying carpets."

The moon was O.K. Kind of boring but pleasant enough. Vast, expansive, like Wyoming at midnight.

We hiked for 3 days to the North Pole of the moon, climbed into a sleeping volcano and took an elevator to the heart of the moon.

The heart of the moon was a power plant carved from one giant beautiful black diamond, it was called El Diamante Negro. From there we took a shuttle train to a planet called Shiraz. Khadija had been here before many times before, in fact she had first conceived of the place in a state of deep meditation and she had meditated so hard that it became a real place. I think I may have even helped build it too matterfact. She gave me the guided tour.

"This is The Joys, sort of a Brazilian vibe," she said, "a lot of clubs here, a lot of discos, if u want to cop some psychedelics, this is the spot."

"I'm straight for now but good lookin' out."

"This is God's Park. Financial District. Downtown, iridescent, abalone shell."

"No doubt."

"This is The Prism."

We found ourselves in a rainbow labyrinth, we wandered, got hella lost. It was hours before we found ourselves in an expansive garden.

"This is The Gardens."

"Tight."

We climbed into a swan shaped boat and rolled along a serene river gazing at lilies and such. Fatima climbed into my arms and fell asleep. Khadija rested her head on my shoulder. Shiraz was a beautiful city. All those years of meditation had really paid off.

39.

"I don't wana be a player no more," said Riffs. We were at a picnic table next to the taco truck at La Raza grocery store in Richmond.

"Ur not a player, u just fuck a lot."

"I'm ready to settle down, get a wife."

"Do it."
"No prospects."
"What about-"
"Nah," cut me off.
"Oh word?"
"Yea, naw."
"U miss her?"
"Hella."
"I'm sure y'all could work it out."
"Eh…"
He didn't seem so confident of that.
"Life sucks man."
I couldn't really argue with that.
"Everything is either sad or infuriating or boring."
"There is joy and peace within. U can unlock it with meditation and whatnot."
"I'm no good at that shit."
"How bout drugs?"
"No good at that either."
"Drinking?"
"I'm too good at that."
"I'll drink to that."
Swigged our cervezas.
It was sunny and nice out.
"Hey at least it's nice out."
"Yeah."

There's no secret. Life iz 2 b lived. Things occur and u occur back to the things, which then occur back to u and so forth. It's not hard. Feelings are just electrical signals in the brain, messages to be heeded, nothing to get worked up over. People wallow in sadness but they really should wallow in joy.

"Cheer up mane."

"O.K."

He didn't cheer up. Or maybe he did later, but I wasn't around. Wished him the best, regardless.

40.

I was at one of those hipster parties in Brooklyn u might have heard about. I was stoned off a weed cookie and on some shrooms. I had tipped some Molly into my champagne glass. It was a warehouse some bands with guitars were playing.

I sniffed some cocaine off some mirror in some room. Some rich and famous fools was there. A number of friends and acquaintances were there. I was vibing, having fun, walking from flower to flower like a bee. Ran into Magic and Elvin.

"Sup."

"Sup."

"Sup."

"How's the album?"

They were working on an album together. Rock and roll music.

"Beautiful."

"I bet."

"U gota hear it."

"I'm in town for two more days man leme slide thru the studio tomoro."

"Fsho."

We went and watched the band. They were called The Real Fake Dead Ghosts. Three white dudes (wait the singing guitarist was half Chinese my bad) playing mellow guitar rock with few changes. Minimal, echoey, not bad in fact pretty O.K.

We caught a cab to Down There in the SouthEast Village. Hi Five and White Dog were there. Quimby was bartending, just giving drinks away. We all got fucked up, I don't think a single dollar was transacted. The talk was open and real and honest and shitty and embarrassing and funny enough and occasionally interesting on an objective level. It was beautiful conversation. I wouldn't even know how to begin to convey it here, even tho I guess I'm supposed to because that's what ur supposed to do in a novel right? That's why people write novels right? Or matter fact why do people write novels? Why am I writing this one? Who cares?

We went to White Dog's friend's apartment, it was some folks over there I never met but they all seemed nice, a couple girls were dancing to the Talking Heads. We drank wine and smoked weed and had a slightly more casual, less acrobatic conversation here, a mellow, good one, effective, adequate for public consumption, we coulda sold that convo for some money, maybe somebody even did.

Morning occurred somehow and we were over at the studio listening to Magic and Elvin's album. Really it was Elvin's album but Magic was at the boards and adding his crucial energy. The album was, just as they had advertised and I had suspected, beautiful, probably as good as the conversation, really just the same conversation continued.

It felt like the room was glowing. The music was hyper real. We listened to the whole album twice then threw on some Miles, smoked a joint.

Arkady, Mali and Piano slid thru with cognac and more tree and we listened to Elvin's album two more times, then some Bud Powell.

Khadija and Fatima rolled thru with some acid.

We all dropped acid except for Khadija and Fatima.

Listened to the Beatles then Migos.

Listened to more Miles.

Then more Migos.

Listened to Magic and Elvin's album again.

Listened to the The Melvins, Yachty, Solange. Listened to Santana, listened to Paul Butterfield, Cannonball Adderley, Bob Dylan, Muddy Waters, Howlin' Wolf, R.L. Burnside, Leadbelly, Bessie Smith, Nina Simone. We all felt very much in the zone, sitting there, letting time pass, intently gazing into the music, communing psychically.

We forgot briefly about the infinite sorrows of the earth.

41.

I was on a boat in the ocean with a tiger just like that other book Life of Pi. Never read it, heard it's tight.

"Bruh," I called to the tiger.

"Bruh," he hollered back.

"U ever read life of Pi?"
"Naw nigga."
"Yea me neither."
"Yet here we find ourselves, on a boat, u, a dude, and me a tiger."
"Yea funny."
The tiger tried to eat me I was like "Bruh, don't eat me."
He was like, "O.K."
Pause.
I tried to keep the conversation lively.
"What's ur top five rappers?"
Tiger said:

Biggie
Pac
Nas
Rakim
Scarface

"Classic."
"U?"

Pac
40
Cube
Mac Dre
4-Tay

"That's a good one."
It was mathematically sound.
"Top five female rappers?"
Tiger said:

Queen Latifah
MC Lyte

Eve
Lil Kim
Nicki

"True."
"U?"
I said:
Lauryn Hill
M.I.A.
Bahamadia
Missy Elliot
Ladybug

"That's a good one."
"U saw that movie Top Five?"
"Yeah that one go hard."
"Super maney."
"That nigga Chris Rock."
"He a fool. Truly one of the best to ever do it."
"Top Five movies."
I said:
Memorias de Subdesarollo
Killer of Sheep
Blood in Blood Out
Malcolm X
Joan of Arc

"Spike Lee Malcolm X?"
"Yeah."
"Ain't that just called X?"
"Iono."
"1928 Joan of Arc?"

"Yea."
"Tight list."
Tiger said:

Top Five
Boomerang
Touki Bouki
Days of Being Wild
Raisin in the Sun

"Wow, great list."
"That was a freestyle."

42.

"This song sucks."
"Yeah what the fuck is this garbage"
"Don't even dignify it with a name, just change it."
"Yeah fuck that song, erase it from history."
"I like that song."
"Yeah that's song's tight."
"Come to think of it I fuck with this song too."
"Song's O.K."
"Song's whatever."
"Can we change it tho?"
"Yea change it."
The song ended.

Chapter ended abrup-

43.

I was in Atlanta with The Dangler and Shooter Jim, not sure what zone, rolled over to DJ Very Very's bday in some other zone, rich black suburb, house party, all of the girls on the first floor, most of the dudes in the cavernous extended basement, replete with escape tunnels, wine cellar, full bar, record library, recording studio, pool table. We listened to some of Shooter Jim's unreleased music and it was insanely beautiful stuff. Listened to some DJ Very Very stuff and it was also incomparably beautiful. Listened to their stuff together and it was also incredibly beautiful.

The whole listening session we were getting insanely drunk off brown liquor.

I felt insane. Naw actually I felt vividly, acutely, brightly, clearly, soberly, lucidly sane. What's the difference?

They set up a microphone, DJ Very Very put on a beat. I kicked a freestyle:

BOOM SHAKA LAKA
HERE COME THE CHIEF ROCKA
ALLAH JAH RASTAFARI CHANGO CHANGO
YEMAYA YEMAYA CHANGO
CHANGO MANI COTE CHANGO MANI CÔTE
OLLE MASA CHANGO ARA BARI COTE

CHANGO ARABARICOTE ODE MATE ICOTE
ALAMA SOICOTE YE ADA MANICOTE ADA
MANICOTE ARAN BANSONI CHANGO
MANI CÔTE CHANGO ELLE MASA CHANGO
ARAMBSONI CHANGO ARA BARICOTE
ODEMATA ICOTE SONI SORI
Y TODO
JAH RASTAFARI ZION I BABYLON ISRAEL EAST
BERLIN ZIG ZAG ZIG ALLAH JAH RASTA
I SIGNIFY
MY IDEA DO MYSTIFY
THIS IS MY NOVEL UR READING
PEACE ALLAH ZIG ZAG UNIVERSAL
ZIG ZAG ETERNAL NO MUSIC
A GOZAR AND IT DONT STOP
ALLAH JAH RASTA
I HAVE THROWN MYSELF AGAINST THE
WORLD MANE
SOMETIMES WITH TOO MUCH FORCE
AND I APOLOGIZE
I'M A PROFESSIONAL RAPPER AND NOVELIST
THIS IS WHAT UR READING RIGHT NOW ARE
U HAVING FUN?
ENDLESS PIMPIN EQUALS ENDLESS FUNK,
SADLY
THE FUNK IS SAD, STRONG AND BEAUTIFUL,
RESILIENT.
DO NOT APOLOGIZE FOR ME OR MAKE
EXCUSES FOR ME JUST ALLOW ME MY
BREAD AND WATER AND EARTHLY JOYS,
AND SIMPLY LET THIS MAN COOK
SINCERELY URS, MOHAMMAD X

Thunderous applause.

Shooter Jim kicked his verse:

In order for capitalism to continue to rule, any action that threatens the right of a few individuals to own and control public property must be prohibited and curtailed whatever the cost in resources (the international wing of repressive institutions has spent one and one-half trillion dollars since World War II), whatever the cost in blood (My Lai, Augusta, Georgia, Kent State, the Panther trials, the frame-up of Angela Davis)! The national repressive institutions (police, National Guard, army, etc.) are no less determined. The mayors that curse the rioters and the looters (Mayor Daily of Chicago has ordered them summarily executed in the streets) ignore the fact that their bosses have looted the world!!!!

Thunderous applause, tears.

Sent it to the homie in LA to get it mixed.

Got back to drinking and bullshitting.

The track did well, we made some money off it, the kids learned they lil lessons.

44.

I was watching the Warriors beat the Cavs at Big Maf's spot in Rodeo City. Riffs and The Dangler were there too. Maf's girl was out in Hawaii w/ the kids, he was headed out the next morning, waiting on some mail or something.

We had on Barter 7.
Smoking hella weed drinking beers.
"U ever read Life of Pi?" I asked Maf.
"Nah, u?"
"Nah."
I asked Maf: "Top Five Rappers"
He said:

E-40
Ghostface
Styles P
Scarface
Cube

"True."

Dangler:
Cube
Rakim
Scarface
40
Biggie

Riffs said:

Too Short
E-40
Chuck D
Phil Lynott
Lemmy Kilmister

I repeated my list from Chapter 41.
We discussed it a bit and finessed a collective Top Five:

E-40
Ice Cube

Scarface
Ghostface
Too Short

Thus the strange soul of democracy yielded extra-emotional intricacies of logic to ponder, mane.

And that is what's known as killing time.

45.

I was in the confessional booth at Notre Dame de Victoire Cathedral goin' off:

"My sins include lust, wrath, greed, sloth, mild gluttony, what else? Oh yeah, pride… I don't think envy. No wait, I envy the good so yeah, the whole biblical milieu as the French say."

"What, u rehearsed that?" Said father So-and-so.

"No, I'm an eloquent man and a genius, just happen to be sinful in the eyes of ur Catholic God."

"Who's ur God."

"Same one I guess, but also plus me. And everybody else."

"No doubt, do a rosary, they got free ones in the basket up front right now for Lent."

"O.K."

I stepped out the booth, lit a candle for Maria y todo sprinkled some holy water on the fo'head went got some duck in Chinatown.

Drank a Tsing-Tao.

Drove around, I had the 88 black Cadillac Seville today, I threw on a Fela Kuti CD Khadija had copped for me at a used clothes store, smoked a KOOL.

Fuck, forgot to snatch a rosary. How it go, Hail Mary full o grace the Lord is with thee, blessed art thou amongst women and blessed be the fruit o thy womb Jesus. Holy Mary Mother of God Pray for our Sinners now and at the hour of our death. Amen. No wait it was like COME WITH ME! HAIL MARY NIGGA RUN QUICK SEE! WHAT DO WE HAVE HERE NOW! NIGGAS WANA RIDE OR DIE! LADADADADADADADADA!

I ended up at a giant, spectacular marble Mausoleum in Paradise Hills. It looked beautiful like a Hitchcock movie. It was hella quiet in there, echoing footsteps and whatnot.

Why was I here? Musta been the Hail Mary. The technology was on par with the flying carpet and the Eagle. I was facing death and loving it, seeing it as an extension of life. I wept. I begged myself for forgiveness.

46.

I was at the crib in Santa Sirena off some Mexican pain killers and some white wine Malika had bought when they were here. Fatima was asleep, Khadija was painting the walls a beautiful vibrant electric neon blue. I was lying on a couch in the middle of the room listening to Ray Charles. The record just said Ray Charles on it and it was a picture of Ray Charles. Beautiful record.

I walked over to my painting studio and started a painting.

I started with yellow, then, light blue, then, dark blue, played with line and gesture, it wasn't looking so good, some pink and a little more dark blue, looked a lil better, lil more yellow and light blue, started looking wack again, etc. finally finished it, it was perfect, insanely beautiful, divine, sublime, a true work or of art, a masterpiece, definitely my greatest and most powerful painting yet. Flawless. I walked it down to the beach and threw it in the ocean. Bruh, I was putting in work today.

Went and got a beer at the ex pat bar, they were watching Ghost on the TV. Whoopi Goldberg, Demi Moore and Patrick Swayze. An all star cast. Dude Josue rolled up to ur boy from across the room, said "Yo vivo aqui y yo trabajo aqui y te prometo, no vas a tener ningun problema con nadie en este campo."

"Muchisima Gracia mano."

There was a big ass jar of tequila that had a preserved rattlesnake in it, the bartender Tino, ladled it into giant shot glasses and handed it to everybody. We all raised our glasses:

"Salúd."

"Santí."

"Cheers."

"Here! Here!"

"¡Orale!"

"¡Olé!"

"¡Ayayay!"

It was actually wild smooth. Went back to beers, they were talking movie trivia, Demi Moore movies.

Sat and drank a couple more beers went back to the crib. The painting was done and it looked beautiful. I made love to my wife and fell asleep.

47.

Fatima's Cosmic Flying Carpet was complete and we all boarded for its first flight.

It was her piloting the thing, Lupe and Rosa co-piloting, Maria, Maestro Karim Hakim Hakim Karim Allah, Khadija and me.

3, 2, 1 BOOM we were flying, the thing flew smooth, it was a sleek stallion, those blueprints were true, the loom executed them flawlessly, we zipped towards the moon at a spectacular pace, were there in like 3 minutes. Dipped into the sleeping volcano at the top and ducked down into El Diamante Negro, shot on thru to Planet Shiraz, cartwheeled across The Joys and God's Park, zig zagged thru the rainbow mazes of the Prism, hit tight ones in The Gardens. My girl had built a beast.

When we landed back in Santa Sirena, Fatima announced she was planning on building an eagle next. She ran off with Lupe and Rosa to their lil clubhouse to start drawing up the blueprints.

We drank some tequila, watched I Love Lucy.

"Man, that carpet's great," I told Khadija.

"It's perfect." She said.

"We gota get an apartment in The Gardens."

"Let's go looking for one tomorrow."

"O.K."

Maestro Hakim said: "What a blessing to have such ingenious children."

"Mashallah," said Khadija.

The night passed into day.

We hit the beach the next day, me, wife n' chile. It was calm, low tide, warm out. I swam around in the ocean while Khadija and Fatima stayed mostly on shore taking the occasional dip.

We went and got tacos at Francisco's.

We came back and watched Betty Boop cartoons. Fatima fell asleep early, a rare occasion. We fell asleep early too. We all met up in a dream where we repeated the exact same day's events again, it was a highly enjoyable dream.

48.

I was in LA at some venue called the Wood Barn Church on Sunset Boulevard, I was fully stupid high off government strength cannabis candies. I felt like weed itself. Nino and Kuumba were there on tour, I had stopped by to sit in. The green room was all jokes, high theater.

I was humming with prismatic power, I felt crystalline. The whole block was electric. I felt metanoid, magnanimous, effervescent, based, ready to go, a live wire, we smoked many blunts, got drunk, put a trumpet mute on the whole night.

I felt self-serious, wonderful.

I focused my energies on being very cool and in turn felt very cool.

I felt very par excellence, whatever that means.

I recited mysterious mutations of immortal poetry throughout the building, it was litty.

I did not give a fuck then and even now at the time of writing this, I do not give a fuck.

There were, at the time, no fucks to be given and it remains at present moment to be the case that the Fucks To Be Given Count has not exceeded zero.

The night carried on, various clowns and soldiers marched to and fro, u could almost get them mixed up. Every clown is, at the bottom of his heart, a soldier. And to be sure, every soldier has something of a clown in him. Bruh.

Cut over to a karaoke bar where I saw Art Max, his girl Waella and her friend Anita and Bruh Bruh Worker and his girl Aria and her friend Symphony, I performed "Don't Stop Believing" to massive applause.

Cut over to a 24 hour diner on Hollywood, had a medium rare steak a glass of bourbon and a glass of water.

I got a cab over to Medina's spot where Khadija and Fatima were already asleep. I curled up next to them.

49.

Mullah X stood outside the liquor store on San Pablo and 30 something, proclamating. Today's sermon was on the topic of Nothing:

WE COME FROM NOTHING ARE NOTHING AND GO TO NOTHING. EVERYTHING IS NOTHING, NOTHING IS EVERYTHING. ALL WE KNOW IS NOTHING. NOTHING UPON NOTHING. NOTHING BEYOND NOTHING. NOTHING MORE THAN NOTHING. ALL THINGS ARE NOTHING. THERE IS NO THING, NO SUCH THING AS NOTHING AND, AS SUCH, NO NOTHING. NOTHING BUT NOTHING. NOTHING WITH NOTHING, ALONGSIDE NOTHING. NOTHING WORTH WORTH NOTING. NOTHING OF INTEREST. NADA. ZIP, ZERO, ZILCH. NOTHING. NO HAY NADA. NADA QUE NADA. NADA POR NADA. NADA, NADA, NOTHING. ¡AYAYAY! NOTHING! ALLAH JAH NADA JAH JAH ALLAH CHANGO! HERE WE ARE SUPER CHARGED AND BRIMMING WITH LOVE AND TOE

TO TOE WITH NOTHING GAZING INTO NOTHING WATCHING NOTHING GAZE BACK. TRUTH IS NOTHING AND NOTHING IS THE TRUTH. THE TRUTH SPRINGS FROM THE CRACKS OF NOTHING AND NOTHINGS SPRING FROM THE CRACKS OF TRUTH. A WINDING VINE, A COMBINING WEB OF NOTHING AND WHAT ELSE BUT NOTHING? THE BLACK NOTHING, THE BLACK DARKNESS, THE WHITE DARKNESS, INFINITY INCORPORATED, WE FACE THE BIG BLACK EVERYTHING WITH LOVE IN OUR HEARTS, THE BIG WHITE NOTHING WITH EVERYTHING IN OUR HEARTS. LOVE IS EVERYTHING. EVERYTHING IS NOTHING. LOVE NOTHING. EMBRACE NOTHING. NOTHING IS EVERYTHING, EMBRACE EVERYTHING. EVERYTHING IS LOVE AND LOVE IS EVERYTHING. LOVE EVERYTHING.

He really turned it around there at the end, gave 'em the ol' zig zag zig. The crowd of listeners, mostly fools exiting the liquor store, nodded, affirmitated, upped, yupped, yessed, truthed, mm-hmmed, snapped, clapped, jazz'd & joon'd in approval.

Mullah X had a sidekick with him today, Young Brother Oscar, handing out some pamphlets he had made.

I had just come across them by chance, I had been walking out the liquor store too, had some henn dog, was headed over to Sandy's to watch the fight, invited Mullah X and Young Brother Oscar, they came along.

It was the usual scene at Sandy's but Sandy had just come into the possession of a big ass flat screen TV so she installed cable and ordered the fight.

It was Sweet Derrick Jones, black dude out of Oakland, and Noah McHurley, white dude out of Pittsburgh.

The rule with boxing is always bet on the dude with the darkest skin and if they both match, the one closest to ur home town, so it was obvious who to root for and so that's what I did. I won a hundred bucks. The fight was for the most part kind of boring and technical but there were some nice lil combos towards the end when McHurley started getting tired, sweet Derrick saw the win coming in the last couple rounds and started putting some flare on things. I was drunk by then and knew I had a hundred bucks coming to me so I was feeling good. Riffs was feeling less good, he had bet on the white guy. A quadroon, his other 3 quarters had got to him. A rare occurrence actually.

After the fight we got into some serious drinking, Mullah X and Young Brother Oscar cut out.

Still wanting to watch the big ass brand new TV, we put on a movie, The Hustler, Paul Newman. We switched to whiskey, blew some trees. Good movie. Put on some Peter Tosh. Khadija slid thru, she had left Fatima with Malika in Sunset City. We watched another movie, one called Love is Colder Than Death, directed by brilliant and famous German speed freak Werner Rainier Fassbinder. Real art joint. It started to rain. We watched another German movie. Werner Herzog's Aguirre: Wrath of God. Crazy movie. Pretty long too. By the time it was over the rain had let up and we headed over to the spot in Paradise Hills (we had been subletting it while in Santa Sirena and it was open for a bit so we had decided to come back to the bay for a little baycation).

Paradise Hills was much how we had left it. A coffee shop had closed. Another one had opened, etc. We put Fatima 2 bed and noodled around on the couch smoochin and what-not, fell asleep. Woke up, smashed, fell asleep.

50.

I went up 2 Seattle on some business, Khadija and Fatima stayed in the Bay. I had a burger at Peter's, their burgers still went hard. Got some oysters and beers with the homies Jimbo and Bready. Bready had a kid now, showed me some pictures. Cute kid.

Mali and Violin were in town too. Linked up with them at an Ethiopian bar, got nice off honey wine and beer, spirits was high.

Seattle, mane. Good town. Lush with greenery, hugging the sweet cold ocean, proper city, novel architecture, the Space needle, viney suburbs. Seahawks mane. Helluva football team. Recent Super Bowl champs. Marshawn Lynch from the town too. Not Seattle, I mean Oakland. Fools from Seattle like to call Seattle The Town but we all know Oakland is The Town. But it's whatever, that's probably the single solitary grievance one could air about Seattle. That and the rain.

Seattle's tight man, Jimi Hendrix, Bruce Lee stayed out there for a second too right? Nirvana... Seattle fools do they thang.

We were posted up in the Ethiopian bar and it was raining hella hard out. Jimbo and Bready had peaced out, it was just me and Mali and Violin now.

"So y'all moved to Mexico?" Said Violin.

"Yea, we still got the Paradise Hills spot too tho, headed back there tomorrow morning."

"No doubt," said Mali.

"We're in the bay for a minute, slide thru and visit."

"We will mane," said Mali.

"Let's go now," said Violin.

"Oh word yeah I got a three legged eagle parked outside right now."

"That's what's up, pause."

We finished our drinks and went outside. The three legged eagle clasped us in each of his talons and flew us down to Paradise Hills. It was hecka quick like 15 minutes. We gazed down at the Pacific coast terrain racing underneath us.

When we got to the crib, Fatima was asleep and Khadija and Malika were drinking tea in the living room describing their dreams to each other.

Khadija put on a new pot of tea and prepared a hookah. Mali put on Love Supreme and I rolled a joint. Violin described her dream from last night:

"Fatima had built me an Eagle. We flew to Haiti and landed on a beach. We sat looking at the waves. My mama came walking out the water and sat down and watched the waves with us. Then my grandmama came walking out the water and we ran up to her and hugged her. Fatima jumped on the Eagle and flew away. And I had breakfast with my mama and grandmama."

"Beautiful dream," said Malika.

"Fatima is very active in the dream realm," I said.

After tea and hookah and records, Khadija led a group meditation. We sat breathing in tranquil silence diving deep into ourselves for countless hours. Our energies combined and harmonized with the universe.

Around dawn, Mali and Violin fell into deep yogic sleep on the rug. I went to the bedroom soon after and fell into deep yogic sleep too and Khadija and Malika went back to describing their dreams to each other.

51.

Shooter Jim and Jammy Mel were performing at the Evil Eye Music Festival on Treasure Island, they had thrown me and Khadija on the list. We dropped Fatima with Munda and headed over, munching on some shrooms in the Yurple Mitsubishi Eclipse. We tried to go in thru the artist entrance in the back and were told to go to the Will Call tent in front.

Khadija groaned acrimoniously: "Ugh, gen pop."

I tried calling their tour DJ, DJ Glasses McGotem, he didn't pick up.

We headed around to the front. The festival goers were in full regalia, it was a regular Mardi Gras.

The Will Call tent didn't have our names, I tried calling Glasses again, still no answer.

I pulled a picture of myself from my pocket. It was a beautiful photograph. I was nude, riding a brown horse. I showed the photograph to the Will Call lady, she called over two of her managers who also inspected the photograph. After some deliberation they handed us two general admission tickets. It was a start.

We walked in and wandered over to the VIP section and sweet talked our way into there but were stopped as we tried to continue on to the artist encampment. I called DJ Glasses again, no answer, called Shooter Jim, no answer, called Jammy Mel, no answer. I saw DJ Glasses McGotem walk by and shouted to him: "Glasses!" He looked over, "Hey man!" He told security,"It's okay they're with me." He held up his laminated badge. "Wrong badge," said security. They were sticklers here. He went to get the tour manager, came back five minutes later with Trip, the ™, he let us pass thru with his special laminated badge. We flipped the security dude the bird and blew raspberries.

Back in the artist area we got some free vodka lemonade and smoked blunts with Shooter Jim, Jammy Mel, DJ Glasses McGottem, DJ Big Mystery, DJ Zippo Quippo, Rap Man Steve and The Dangler.

"How u get in here?" I asked The Dangler.

"I don't know man."

A dude came in and interviewed Shooter Jim and Jammy Mel. They were in rare form, cutting up, all aces, stickin and movin, tag teamin, quick jabs, a show in and of itself.

On the way out the interviewer asked me if I was KOOL MAN. I told him no, I was MOHAMMAD X. He shrugged and left.

It was time for Shooter Jim and Jammy Mel to hit the stage, we all followed along en masse. Bruh, it was lit, some truly transcendent shit. The crowd was super duper hyphy, they were going bonkers mane, they were nuts. The sun was setting over the gorgeous Alcatrazian skyline and the light was just so. Shooter and Jammy had seen a lot of success of late and it was all well deserved. A truly special experience, enlightening, gave me some life.

Afterward we all climbed into the tour bus for more vodka lemonades and blunts. Shooter and Jammy were tired and about to conk out. They were headed to LA that night. We bid them farewell and peaced.

Gave The Dangler a ride home and picked up Fatima.

"She's an angel," said Munda.

"I know right?"

52.

The dawning of the sun that morning was was like the dawning of a million suns, a ganglion of lightnings for my wonder.

We were in Miami at the Hilton (Penthouse suite obv) overlooking the beach. Khadija and Fatima were asleep still and I was at the window with a mimosa soaking it up.

We were gona meet up con mi abuelita, mi Tia Alejandra y mi prima Tina for brunch later on.

Did 100 push-ups and 100 sit-ups then jumped out the window (33rd floor) into the ocean, swam over to Cuba. They knew me there.

"¡ES EL KUL MAN!"

"Ya no, ahora soy MOHAMMAD X."

"¡ES EL MOHAMMAD X."

They brought me to their king, Fidel Castro. We smoked cigars in his expansive library and he told me stories about his baseball days. He was a gifted left handed pitcher in college. The MLB sent down an all star team to play an exhibition game against Havana's best players in an attempt to scout new talent and in that game Fidel gave up no runs when he was on the mound and even struck out Hank Greenberg. His talent caught the attention of the Pittsburgh Pirates, the Washington Senators and the New York Yankees, who started a bidding war to draft him, but he declined in order to lead a Communist Revolution and oust American imperialism from the island for a good half century or so. It was an interesting chat.

I bid the homie adieu and swam back to Miami. Khadija and Fatima were up and ready to go, watching Adventure Time. I jumped in the shower, got dressed and we jumped in the rental (pink Lambo as per Khadija's request) over to Usmail's Cuban Bistro in Hollywood Beach for brunch. It was crackin.

Mi abuelita wasn't the biggest Castro fan for whatever reasons so I declined to mention my lil kick it sesh earlier this morning, we mostly talked about Jose Marti, her favorite poet and favorite topic of discussion.

At one point towards the end of brunch she stood up on her strong, spry, 99 year old legs and recited in full su poema favorita de Marti k se llama Los Zapaticos de Rosa and it went a lil something like this:

Hay sol bueno y mar de espumas, Y arena fina, y Pilar Quiere salir a estrenar Su sombrerito de pluma.

—"Vaya la niña divina!" Dice el padre, y le da un beso, "Vaya mi pájaro preso A buscarme arena fina!"

—"Yo voy con mi niña hermosa", Le dijo la madre buena: "¡No te manches en la arena Los zapaticos de rosa!"

Fueron las dos al jardín Por la calle del laurel: La madre cogió un clavel Y Pilar cogió un jazmín. Ella va de todo juego, Con aro, y balde y paleta: El balde es color violeta, El aro es color de fuego.

Vienen a verlas pasar, Nadie quiere verlas ir, La madre se echa a reír, Y un viejo se echa a llorar.

El aire fresco despeina A Pilar, que viene y va Muy oronda: —"¡Dí, mamá! ¿Tú sabes qué cosa es reina?"

Y por si vuelven de noche De la orilla de la mar, Para la madre y Pilar Manda luego el padre el coche. Está la playa muy linda: Todo el mundo está en la playa: Lleva espejuelos el aya De la francesa Florinda.

Está Alberto, el militar Que salió en la procesión Con tricornio y con bastón, Echando un bote a la mar.

¡Y qué mala, Magdalena Con tantas cintas y lazos, A la muñeca sin brazos, Enterrándola en la arena!

Conversan allá en las sillas, Sentadas con los señores, Las señoras, como flores, Debajo de las sombrillas.

Pero está con estos modos Tan serios, muy triste el mar: Lo alegre es allá, al doblar, En la barranca de todos!

Dicen que suenan las olas Mejor allá en la barranca, Y que la arena es muy blanca Donde están las niñas solas.

Pilar corre a su mamá: —"¡Mamá, yo voy a ser buena; Déjame ir sola a la arena; Allá, tú me ves, allá!"

—"¡Esta niña caprichosa! No hay tarde que no me enojes: Anda, pero no te mojes Los zapaticos de rosa.

Le llega a los pies la espuma, Gritan alegres las dos; Y se va, diciendo adiós, La del sombrero de pluma.

¡Se va allá, donde ¡muy lejos! Las aguas son más salobres, Donde se sientan los pobres, Donde se sientan los viejos!

Se fue la niña a jugar, La espuma blanca bajó, Y pasó el tiempo, y pasó Un águila por el mar.

Y cuando el sol se ponía Detrás de un monte dorado, Un sombrerito callado Por las arenas venía.

Le llega a los pies la espuma, Gritan alegres las dos; Y se va, diciendo adiós, La del sombrero de pluma.

¡Se va allá, donde ¡muy lejos! Las aguas son más salobres, Donde se sientan los pobres, Donde se sientan los viejos!

Se fue la niña a jugar, La espuma blanca bajó, Y pasó el tiempo, y pasó Un águila por el mar.

Y cuando el sol se ponía Detrás de un monte dorado, Un sombrerito callado Por las arenas venía.

Anoche soñó, soñó Con el cielo, y oyó un canto, Me dio miedo, me dio espanto, Y la traje y se durmió".

"Con sus dos brazos menudos Estaba como abrazando; Y yo mirando, mirando Sus piececitos desnudos.

"Me llego al cuerpo la espuma. Alcé los ojos, y ví Está niña frente a mí Con su sombrero de pluma.

—"¡Se parece a los retratos Tu niña!"—dijo:—"¿Es de cera? ¿Quiere jugar? ¡si quisiera!... ¿Y por qué está sin zapatos?"

Mira, ¡la mano le abrasa, Y tiene los pies tan fríos! ¡Oh, toma, toma los míos, Yo tengo más en mi casa!

¡No sé bien, señora hermosa, Lo que sucedió después; ¡Le ví a mi hijita en los pies Los zapaticos de rosa!

Se vio sacar los pañuelos A una rusa y a una inglesa; El aya de la francesa Se quitó los espejuelos.

Abrió la madre los brazos, Se echó Pilar en su pecho, Y sacó el traje deshecho, Sin adornos y sin lazos

Todo lo quiere saber De la enferma la señora: ¡No quiere saber que llora De pobreza una mujer!

—"¡Sí, Pilar, dáselo! ¡y eso También! ¡tu manta! ¡tu anillo!" Y ella le dio su bolsillo, Le dio el clavel, le dio un beso.

Vuelven calladas de noche A su casa del jardín; Y Pilar va en el cojín De la derecha del coche.

Y dice una mariposa Que vio desde su rosal Guardados en un cristal Los zapaticos de rosa.

She sat back down and took a sip of cafe. The entire restaurant burst into deafening applause. The waiter brought out free flan for our table.

53.

I was on a date with my beautiful bride KHADIJA X, rolling thru the skreets of Los Angeles in a lemon yellow 2002 Corvette convertible listening to Future.

The city was excitedly assembling itself alongside us as we rolled along, an anarchy of magicks, a palm fronded bazaar turistical, a casino of lawns, palm trees, mini malls, Spanish architecture.

The sky was neon blue, vibracious white clouds galloping across the sky, electric zens rumbled thru a young player's domepiece, a veritable psychedelic garden of delights sprang forth on the film reels of our eyeballs, we zipped thru the super hyphy cinematic dreamscape of The Angels

We was toe up. I was hitting corners like SKREE! SKRT!

Fatima was at Medina's spot, they were bedazzling matching jean jackets.

We hit Urasawa got some Toro sashimi and sake, lamped there.

Hopped back in the whipper drove up to the Hollywood sign, posted up in the second O, gazed at the sprawling metropo sparkling like a chest o jewels. Amazing stuff.

"Feel like I got Dejavu."

"Me too."

"Maybe this has happened before."

"In a universe of infinite possibilities, it almost certainly has."

"Infinite times probably, huh."

We thought on that.

She said: "Nothing is impossible."

I said: "True."

"So then, what do u want to do?"

"I guess this."

"You guess?"

"I mean we're here now so this must be where we're supposed to be."

"Yeah, but how do u feel?"

"It doesn't seem to matter how I feel."

"Nothing matters, I just want to know how u feel."

"I feel good."

"Me too."

We kizzed.

54.

Fatima finished construction on her eagle. She was a beaut. She called her Fatima 2. The eagle was made of pure gold sourced from Ghana. It had twelve gleaming golden talons and a giant golden heart pumping golden blood to its golden organs. It breathed carbon dioxide thru the nostrils of its golden beak and into its massive golden lungs, and exhaled oxygen. It was powered by the sun and the human emotion of wonder. It had seven eyes made of rubies and a secret eighth eye on its heart.

We boarded. It was me, Khadija, Hakim and Maria with Fatima, Lupe and Rosa at the Helm.

We flew to Shiraz again and kicked it there all day, ended up spending the night at a nice lil hotel in The Gardens.

The next day, we boarded the Golden Eagle again and flew to The Pain.

The Pain was 999 light years away. It was a giant spherical mirror, we landed on its surface and realized it had the consistency of quicksand. We sank to the core of The Pain, found ourselves surrounded by liquid mirror. We became one with The Pain. We became The Pain. The Pain was us and we were the Pain.

The Pain is basically a black hole, u get sucked in, it's made out of everything that it sucks in, u can never leave The Pain. We were stuck in The Pain forever and could never leave. It was unsparing of everyone, man, woman and child. We didn't know that when we went there or else we probably wouldn't have gone there. That's pretty much how everybody gets there I guess.

I don't know who's idea it was to go to The Pain, I don't think it matters tho, what matters was we were somehow all drawn to The Pain collectively as a group and now we were all in it, we were in The Pain and we were The Pain. The Pain was in us, The Pain was us.

There was no way out of The Pain but nothing is impossible so there was a way out of The Pain. We looked to the kids to figure it out. They were younger and their brains were fresher and more pliant, less used to and inclined to trust the strictures and concretisms of our continued existence over time, the constant kowtowing to some so-called objectivity. If anyone could figure the zany quantum secrets of The Pain it was the kids.

Oh, BTW, speaking of kids, a couple chapters back I forgot to mention Khadija had given birth to those twins she had been pregnant with. A boy and a girl. Fausto and Madonna. They were hella quiet, that's why u din't hear much from them. But they were there in The Pain too, and yung as they were, they proved indispensable for our escape.

"Just think, Fatima," Fausto coached Fatima. "Nothing is impossible, everything is possible."

Madonna chimed in: "We are The Pain and The Pain is us. To escape from The Pain we must abandon The Self."

Fatima thought about it, she conferred with Lupe and Rosa for a few minutes until finally, Rosa, the quieter of the two twin sisters, spake:

"There is no Pain."

And just like that we were all on the deck in Santa Sirena looking at the night sky hanging over the beautiful roaring ocean. All it took was the psychic energy of four twins. We had escaped would could be classified as a Four Twin Pain.

Some echo of The Pain lingered in all of us, but we were home safe.

We all said gracias to Rosa.

Me and Maria and Maestro Hakim Karim Allah drank some Tequila, then Maria and Karim Hakim cut out with Lupe and Rosa.

Fausto y Madonna walked in with hella cups of tea for everybody on a big tea tray. These kids really did they thang.

"Where's ur Eagle, Fatima?" asked Khadija.

"Who cares?" said Fatima.

55.

I was in the Regal (1983, Root Beer Brown) whipping thru Philly headed to Regal Cinemas at Moorestown Mall in Cherry Hill, New Jersey to catch The Revenant, it was the closest theater playing it at the moment. Always been a big Leo D'Cap fan and this was supposed to be the one that would finally win him that Oscar that always eluded him. I had finished my business in town, pretty stoned and buzzed off some dark liquids and was killing time before catching a flying carpet back to Santa Sirena (Fatima 2, The Golden Eagle, was still M.I.A.)

I had on the new Freeway tape it wasn't bad. I had just visited an old buddy in Westpark, I had about $20k in cash in a duffel in the trunk feeling just a touch nervous but stopped at a Crown Fried anyway cause I was hella hungry got a 4 piece (arm, leg, leg, arm) a biscuit, fries and a ginger ale, ate in the car. Finished the new Freeway, put on the latest Meek Mill. It was tight.

Drove over to Cherry Hill stopped in Z Mitchell's in Merchantville for some henn to drink at the movies. Rolled a white owl and smoked it in the car outside the liquor sto' put on the last Slaughterhouse tape mashed over to the Moorestown Regal and went in. I had missed some previews, I hate that, they're one of my favorite things about the movies. A trailer for the new Star Wars started and I had seen it hella times so I jogged to get some popcorn.

The blonde girl handing me the bag of popcorn said: "Are u KOOL MAN?"

I said: "No, I'm MOHAMMAD X."

She said: "Oh."

I made it back as the movie started, it was O.K.

Went a little too hard on the Henny and fell asleep.

Fatima 2, The Golden Eagle, visited me in my dreams, said: "Ay!"

"What?"

"Hop aboard."

I hopped aboard, surfed along, we zipped thru elaborate, palatial cloud patterns until we ended up back at the crib at Santa Sirena Madonna y Fausto lampin' watching Kiki's Delivery Service, wifey takin a nap.

Fatima come running out the house like: "Oh my God u found Fatima 2!"

I said: "No, I didn't, this is just a dream."

Fatima said: "Life is just a dream."

She had me there. We called over Maestro Karim Hakim Allah and Maria, they slid thru with Lupe and Rosa who immediately departed from they guardians and jumped on Fatima 2 along with Fatima (1) and they shot into outer space off to Allah knows where.

"How was Philly?" asked Maestro.

"O.K. Little boring just ended up going to the movies by myself after all was said and done."

"Whatchu see?"

"The Revenant."

"Any good?"

"Fell asleep. Might still be asleep actually."

"La Vida Es Sueña," remarked Maria.

"Ya tu sabe," I said.

Fuck, I had left $20k cash in the duffel in the trunk of the Root Beer Brown '83 Regal outside the Moorestown Mall Regal in Cherry Hill!

I called up the homie Jorge who had been crashing at his girl's spot in Hi Nella, not too far from Cherry Hill.

"Bruh, I'ma ask u a big favor for which I will reward u handsomely."

"U had me at reward."

"I need u to catch a ride over to the Regal Cinemas at Moorestown Mall in Cherry Hill, find a Root Beer Brown '83 Regal in the P. lot, crack that bitch open and hotwire it, drive it down to Santa Sirena, Mexico. There's 20 racks in the trunk, bring me 10 and u can have the other half for gas money and ur troubles."

"Fair enough deal."

It was a generous deal. Dude was butt ass broke and leaning on his girl way too hard. With 10 stacks he could afford to buy himself some new pants in the relationship. It was water to me. Nada.

Pero todo es nada si tu quiere get real widdit.

Anyway, I never saw Jorge again, bless his worthless soul. Nigga bought himself two pairs of pants it seems.

56.

"Anything."

I was at my white people bar in downtown SF.

The bartender brought me a shot of Bulleit and an Anchor Steam, I threw back the shot and chased it with a sip of beer.

"Nother court date?"

"Yep. Ay my fault, I don't know if I ever learned ur name."

"Phil."

"I'm MOHAMMAD X."

"Cheers."

He walked away to wash a cup or something.

Emperor Norton was there again.

"Ur always here."

"Look who's talking."

"How's Peruvian Rice?"

"Terrible, but looking up."

"I have faith man."

"That's the spirit."

I hit the court house, the old wizard judge was off today, in his place a heavy Mexican lady with a stern look in her bespectacled eye.

"Where's ur lawyer?" She asked.

"She's absent again, I'm representing myself."

"That's within ur legal right but out of curiosity, did u pass the bar?"

"Yea, on my way over, I had a shot of Bulleit and an Anchor Steam."

The stenographer rolled her eyes.

The judge said: "Is the nature of man to sin?"

I said: "Nay!"

"Then what is the origin of sin?"

"The devil planted his seed in the Garden of Eden."

"What is the origin of the devil?"

"He was a renegade angel what fell from Heaven."

"What's the difference between Heaven and Hell?"

"Location, location, location."

"What is man?"

"Man is 5, Obatala, the throat chakra, power, refinement."

"What is the Devil?"

"The Devil is 6, stronger than man, weaker than God."

"What is God?"

"Allah is Love and Love is Everything."

"What is Everything?"

"Nothing."

"What is Nothing?"

"Who cares?"

"Ur free to go."

"ALLAH CHANGO JAH RASTAFARI!"

I went over to The Future Primitive Art School and caught the chopper back to Santa Sirena with Fatima.

57.

I was riding the train and this Puerto Rican kid said simple and plain "Let's battle."

It kinda took me by surprise. The brother was moving with his eyes on the prize I said, "Screw it, I ain't got nothing to lose so um let me bust this shit right quick so um, hurry up kid bust ur joints and then I'll bust mine."

He said, "O.K. Yo blah blah blo blah," is what he said. Then I came around and just fucked up his head:

ALLAH CHANGO JAH RASTAFARI
HAILE SELLASIE I
ALLAH HU AKBAR
ALHUMDULILLAH
YEMAYA YEMAYA
CHANGO
BABALU AYE
ALLAH
ALLAH
ALL I WANA DO IS ZOOMA ZOOM ZOOM
ZOOM AND A BOOM BOOM
AND TAKE YA MONEY
THE SOFT PINK LITE BETWEEN DAY AND
NITE MAMA
MIRA!
LA ULTIMA ESTRELLA BRAVA K BRILLA EN EL
CIELO SOLITARIO
EL AIRE FRIO
Y YO SOLO YO Y EL CORAZONITO MIO
RIO DE LAGRIMAS PA K
NADA MAS QUE NADA MAMA

NO TENGA K LLORAR
HUMAN CONSCIOUSNESS TETHERED TO
THE UNIVERSAL COSMIC SUPERSOUL
OM SHANTI OM ALLAH CHANGO JAH
INFINITY IS REALITY
FINITY IS INCONCEIVABLE
THE ARROW OF TIME IS A QUIRK OF HUMAN
PERCEPTION
SCIENCE IS A CLUMSY POETRY
WORDS ARE COMPUTERS OF THE MIND
CRYSTALS ARE LVIING CREATURES THAT
HAVE MADE HOMES IN HUMAN
APPLIANCES
ANIMAL VEGETABLE AND MINERAL SHARE
CONSCIOUSNESSES
THE MULTITUDE OF BEINGS ARE AT ONCE A
SINGLE BEING
THE TRICKERIES AND SPECIFICITIES OF MAN
ARE A TRIFLE, A DROP, A GRAIN, A MERE
ANNOYANCE
TRUTH TRANSCENDS LANGUAGE
THE BODY IS A HUSK, A VEHICLE
FUCK YO MIXTAPE
BE KIND, REWIND
UR LYRIX IS WACK SUN
PEACE ALLAH
GOD US ETERNAL
UR BARS ARE TRASH AND LACK HEAT
UR POETIX IZ SUB PAR
PEACE IS WITHIN
THE BATTLE IS FICTIONAL
WAR IS EXTINCT

ONCE U REALIZE THIS
PEACE ARISES WITHIN UR SOUL AND
SPREADS TO ALL CORNERS
PEACE ROCKS WAR IN ITS FACE AND STABS
WAR'S BRAIN WITH ITS NOSE BONE
OOH GIRL
GET IT
PEACE KINETIC
SHOTS WILL BE LICKED
LICKS WILL BE HIT
ET CETERA
MY SIXTEENS IS TRIPLE BEAM
MY THIRTY TWOS IS HURTING DUDES
MY SIXTY FOES IS SHITTING ON U SHITTY
HOES
U AINT GOT NO BITCHES I CAN SEE IT IN YA
EYES
JAH IS ETERNAL
PEACE ELECTRIC

The whole train car erupted in magnanimous applause.

The kid started crying.

He got off at the next stop, probably cried all the way home.

See, he thought an emcee who was seen on TV couldn't hold his shit down in the NYC.

58.

I was returning to Santa Sirena from a quick trip over to New York.

Fatima was in the main room at the big oak table working on the blueprints for a rose gold falcon to be named Rosa 2. Looked very beautiful. The sliding door to the deck was ajar and the long white curtains rustled in the mild breeze. It was sunny.

Khadija was on the deck in deep meditation, greasing the cosmic wheel as it were.

They were a perfect pair, made me feel almost obsolete frankly. And I guess I was.

Woman is the future of man. Man will go extinct. The Y chromosome is a dalliance, a brief hiccup in the expansive history of the universe.

I sat next to Khadija and meditated alongside her. She was good at meditating and I think so good at it that it kind of spilled over and made me pretty good at it too. To be fair I think I was decent at it before tho.

We beamed our energy into Fatima as she rendered out the sweet thin blue arcs and curvatures of her falcon.

Seven falcons circled above, overseeing our labor.

The first falcon, Etel, said:

"Love is love, Allah, bless up."

The second falcon, Randa, said:

"Alhumdulillah."

The third falcon, Samar, said:

"Ayy, turn up, turn up."

The fourth falcon, Hawra, said:

"It's lit, betch, yass."

The fifth falcon, Badria, said:
"Aay lmao!"
The sixth falcon, Ahlam, said:
"Allah Hu Akbar, bong bong have a nice dream!"
The seventh falcon, Miral, said:
"No doubt, no doubt."
In unison they skrayed:
"Space is the physicality of love."
Etel said:
"Existence is an invention of the mind."
Randa said:
"Truth is a rag doll."
Samar said:
"Everything is nothing."
Hawra said:
"Who got tree I'm tryna blaze."
Badria said:
"Truth is a hot skillet."
Ahlam said:
"Truth is a basket of eggs."
Miral said:
"No doubt, no doubt."
In unison they yeeked:
"Life impersonates itself."

It was all good stuff, we were all clicking together, humming in unison. A fine day in ol' Mexico. The sun brilliated with tender joy.

59.

I went out walking thru the hills of Santa Sirena. I copped a loosie at the convenient store and sipped at it as I ambled.

Many a succulent, much cacti, various palms, magnolia, wispy willows, birch, feather grass, ice plants with they lil purple flowers, Africanesque daisies, cliff roses, buttress-rooted ficus insipidae, century plants blossoming with aspargal and caulifloral sprigs, houses painted brite blu, brite yelo, brite pinc, brite gring, brite yt, vivid and saturated even as they faded and flaked. The houses thinned and the flora thickened. A rabbit here or there, a fox, a wild eyed coyote. A clear day, touch windy, fresh sea air, the roar of waves against the cliff.

I thought: What is life? Why are we here?

Then I thought: who cares?

I went on my phone and ordered a Dolce & Gabbana abaya for Khadija, some pink and gray Jordan XIII's for Fatima, a six shooter for Fausto, a bundle of Egyptian sage for Madonna and an Iguodala jersey for me.

Mexico mane. Land of mystery. A hawk skreeked, a falcon swooped, a bluebird peeped, alighted 'pon a nopal patch.

I walked to the edge of the scrubby green brush garnished red rock cliff and gazed at the endless gray blue waves churning and lapping and cresting below. A gray whale breached and spouted in the distance, laced me with game. I thought about his life, swammin thru the endless salt-soaked sea, singing his lil gray whale songs. Bruh. What a life.

I felt immense gratitude for the simple fact of my existence. Just to experience this moment of quietude. I thanked the gray whale for the revelation. The animal kingdom is overflowing with wisdom.

I walked along saw a little smiley face painted in yellow on a rock, looked like this:

:)

Cute lil thang.

Walked on.

Tiny yellow wildflowers, weeds in the wrong context but here they were a fine accoutrement.

I walked down a steep rocky slope to the beach. Waves were smashing on the sea smoothed stones, heaving, swelling, gray green blue, crashing, foaming white. Solid stuff.

Gazed at the distant horizon, hazy silver, the sky was blue gray, trinkled with yellow sunlight. Stayed there a while, watching the waves crash and lap.

Climbed back up the incline, walked home.

Khadija was lying on the couch sipping tea. Fatima & Madonna were was taking a nap. Faust was out somewhere getting into trubbs.

"U see the lil smiley I left u?"

"Yea mami, hella cute."

I took a nap.

Woke up and Khadija, and Fatima & Madonna were chanting "Om Shanti Om" and other various Oms.

Maestro Hakim slid thru we chiefed a zooter.

"Where's Maria and the kids?"

"Visiting fam in Tijuana."

"U didn't go?"

"Not a fan of Tijuana, plus I'm not sure if her family likes me."

"What's not to like?"

"Beats me."

Rolled up another doober puff passed it with Khadija while Fatima worked on her rose gold falcon blueprint & Madonna read Donald Duck comix.

The night came and the stars shook they lil asses for us.

60.

I was wandering thru an abandoned hotel in Pennsylvania.

Found myself in an empty ballroom with a big chandelier, had my myself a ball. It was a ball of one. I smoked a cigarette and stared up at the chandelier. A ball it was.

I wandered into a hallway and tinkered with a piano. Played Tea for Two.

I walked over to a decrepit library, looked thru the dusty books.

A red Bible and a blue Bible.

Vice President of the Revolution.

Collected Writings of Bakunin.

Groucho Marx biography written by his son.

Some book called After Life's Fitful Fever They Sleep Well.

A Moveable Feast.

Orientalism, Eddie Said.

Dune.

North American Birds Almanac

Collected Tolstoy.

Not a bad library.

Walked over to the indoor pool. It was filled with water, oddly. Didn't bother to chance a swim tho.

Walked thru the halls, ugly carpet, ice machines here and there.

Came across an open room, went in.

TV was on.

On the TV was a single white dove flying thru a brite blu sky on loop.

I sat at the foot of the bed and watched for an hour, unsure of what to do next.

Where was I? How did I get here? Why was I here? Who cares, I guess.

I realized I was back in The Pain. I was The Pain and The Pain was me.

The dove kept flying, gorgeous and sad in the brite blu sky.

This was The Pain.

Wasn't so bad really.

Walked around some more.

Smoked another cigarette in the ballroom.

Played Tea for Two again.

Went over to the library and flipped thru some Tolstoy, then thru a blue Bible, then thru a red Bible.

Skimmed the Groucho Marx biography, great stuff. What a dude.

This library was missing Jose Marti, I felt.

The Pain is a heady purgatorial chamber. The Pain is O.K., if a little boring.

I hung out in The Pain for hours, days, weeks, months, years, smokin bogies, playing piano, reading, doing push-ups and sit ups.

Eventually, I grew tired of The Pain and discarded Pain Consciousness.

I woke up on the couch in Santa Sirena.

Khadija and the kids were out somewhere prob walking thru the hillz.

I headed over to Maestro Karim Hakim's house down the way. Passed Khadija's little smiley face graffiti rock.

:)

Sweet piece.

A little further along was a painting of a bird in yellow on another rock. Not as good as the smiley face in my opinion.

Walked along some more ran into Khadija, along the cliff, she was with Fatima & Madonna (who knows where Fausto was) and she had a yellow bucket of paint and a brush.

"What did u think of the bird?"

"Not as good as the smiley face."

She chucked the bucket of paint off the cliff into the ocean.

"U didn't have to do all that."

"Oh, but I did."

"I'm headed to Maestro Hakim Karim Allah's to burn a jay u wana come?"

"O.K."

A seagull flew past covered in yellow paint, said "sup." Poor thing musta got hit with the flying paint bucket on its way down, but he didn't seem to be trippin so hey.

We were like "sup" back, he flew up on his way.

Made it over to Maestro's, zooked a zoomer had a nip o' tequila. Maria was still in TJ visiting fam w Lupe and Rosa. 'Tima & 'Donna played with the cats Hypatia & Carlos.

HK/KH played us a song on the guitar. A number called Indio Boracho. I had never heard it before, it was great.

Headed back after a while, passed the little yellow bird painted on the rock.

"Actually I kinda like it."

"Of course u do, it's perfect."
"Sorry to have doubted u."

61.

"U can't win."
"True."
Me and Riffs were drinking beer and eating tacos at La Razon Azteca.
"Life is pain."
"Life is suffering."
"Life is hell."
"Life is shit."
"Life is garbage."
"Life is worthless."
"Waste of time."
"Absolute trash."
"Miserable rat race."
"No way out."
"No exit."
"No escape."
"I want to die."
"I want to blow my brains out with a gun."
"Wish I was never born."
"I'm trash."
"Yeah u are."

"Fuck u, so are u."
"Yeah, so what, fuck u too."
"Life is meaningless."
"Life is a joke."
"I'm garbage."
"Ur a piece of shit."
"Fuck u."
"Fuck u."
"Ur a piece of shit too."
"I am but speak for urself."
"U right u right."
"Dude, life sux."
"Life is a total bummer."
"Everything sucks."
"Everything is wack as fuck."
"Life bites."
"Life sux major D."
"Yeah, man."
"These tacos are pretty good tho."
"Yea."

62.

"I guess I'm dumb but I don't care," I told Khadija. We were sitting on the deck looking at the sky. The kids was asleep.

"U are a moron."

"Ur supposed to assure me that I'm a genius."

"I used to think u were a genius, now I think ur an idiot."

"I had some tacos with Riffo yesterday when I was up in the bay, we were talking about how we're both trash."

"Bro-ing down, I see."

"We were talking about how life sucks."

"It doesn't."

"Yeah, he just got me in a mood. I was in full agreement with the idea yesterday. Today, not so much."

"The heart is a fickle creature."

"Ya tu sabe mami."

We saw a shooting star.

"U see that?"

"Yea."

"Life is pretty cool sometimes."

"There must be some respite to the perpetual suffering that is consciousness."

"Feelings are soon to be extinct probably."

"Maybe."

We sat in silence looking at the moon.

"U ever heard of The Flat Earth Society?"

"No."

"They think the earth is flat."

"Figured as much."

"They say it's a disc, with the North Pole in the center and Antarctica as an ice wall at the edges, surrounding the entire ocean."

"Strangely elegant model."

"Yea they say the sun is like 20 miles across and the moon landing was faked."

"It was."

"Who knows…"
"I do, it was faked."
"O.K."
The ocean waves down at the bottom of the hill shushed and hushed.
"So u think the Earth's flat too then?"
"No it's a tube."
"That's stupid."
"Ur stupid."
"Can't argue with that."
"U heard about the Hollow Earth Theory?"
"Yeah, I think u told me before."
The waves shushed.
"Existence is perception."
"Om shreem hreem Saraswati-ya namaha."
"Hare Krishna, mami."
"Brain Drain."
"B-r-r-rang-dang-dang."
"Subtractive Schooling."
"Berlin…"
"Beijing…"
"Seoul…"
"Mexico City."
"Havana."
"Allah."
"Jah Rasta."
"Chango."
"Yemaya."

63.

"Bonjour."

"Hello."

"How are you?"

"Good mane, u?"

"Jet lag man, tired, give me wine."

"We're out of wine."

"Fuck! Shit!"

"Come on let's go get u some wine."

Felix had arrived from France. He was a classic Frenchman, real asshole, but I liked the guy.

We hit the wine store, found some French wine.

"This wine is shit but at least it's French."

I think I mostly got along with dude cause I thought the accent was funny. Also he was the lean plug. Actually that was the main reason I got along with him.

We bought a case. He was only in town 2 days, subletting a little beach house nearby, still I worried he'd run out of wine. He was a real wine hound.

"I don't understand why Americans love drinking cough syrup so much, u are crazy."

"Brazy," I corrected.

"I don't do that gangster slang bullsheet."

"Relax man, have some more wine."

He did.

I did too.

Khadija had some wine too.

Maestro Hakim Karim Allah swam thru with Maria back from TJ, Lupe and Rosa in tow. They ran off with Fatima and Madonna to start construction on Rosa 2, The Rosegold Falcon.

Fausto was at the casino playing dice.

Maria and Hakim brought tequila but I stuck to wine.

We bullshitted, played a lot of Black Sabbath records, Flower Traveling Band, Hawkwind, Motörhead, Thin Lizzy, Santana, Curtis Mayfield, were into like Bob Dylan and Richie Havens by the morning.

Khadija had gone to bed, Rosa and Lupe had slept over in Fatima and Madonna's room. Faustino was still out shooting dice but I wasn't worried about him, he was strapped. It was just me, Felix, Hakim and Maria drinking, bullshitting, playing records. I dipped into the sizzurp, popped an adderall to keep from nodding off. I was lit. It was lit. Both It and I were lit. Felix had smuggled in some hash too so we were smoking that. That was lit too.

We slept it off the next day and drank all night again the next night, ran out of wine switched to tequila. More lean and speed for me too. Khadija massaged my neck and whispered in my ear, "Easy there, cowboy."

"My fault, my fault, I just never see Felix is all."

"At this rate u might never see him again."

"HardeeHarhar."

The second night we listened to Madonna (the singer, not our daughter, she was off building a flying carpet or a bird or something with her sis and clique), Janet Jackson, Mariah Carey, Whitney Houston, Nina Simone, Smokey Robinson, Ohio Players, Earth Wind and Fire, more Nina Simone. By the end I could barely tell the difference between the sun and the moon. I don't remember any of the conversation but it was all very heartfelt.

Felix cut and I slept for two days, then went on a month long cleanse, no alcohol, no drugs (well, weed but that don't count), a lot of fresh juices and whatnot, I was feeling good. Almost stayed off it all for good but then I went to an old friend's wedding and got tore off champagne and whiskey.

Time passed, the Rosa 2 neared completion.

64.

We were at the crib, Khadija was chanting:

"Om Namoh Bhagavate Vasudevayah"

I was doing push-ups.

Fatima, Madonna, Lupe and Rosa came in and announced that construction on Rosa 2: The Rosegold Falcon was complete. No sooner had they made their announcement than Rosa 2 came swooping down from the electrum tinged clouds, a shrieking missile of perfect beauty.

It was Fatima's best work to date, owed in no small part to the hardworking, industrious and ingenious twins and sharp lil Madonna. Fausto had no part in this. He was still out shooting dice, up a few hunnit bux after going broke and borrowing from his homie Aurelio. But the 4 chix, they were gelling into a nigh perfect, unstoppable quadrangle offense of design and engineering.

We hopped aboard for a ride. Hit the moon, Shiraz, Mars, Venus, even young Pluto. The thing handled like a dream, a true luxury vehicle.

We missed an exit and ended up headed to Planet X. None of us had ever been so we said fuck it and zoomed on.

Planet X is made of solid black obsidian, the dried and cooled magma of a volcanic black hole, one of the many great mysteries of science.

We made it to Planet X, landed next to a black river.

The water on Planet X is black and strong, one sip will hydrate, rejuvenate and energize for a solid year.

We sipped from a black river, it was no joke, powerful stuff, beautiful clear, clean, fresh taste.

Planet X, man, what a destination.

Planet X is home to one of the universe's largest black diamond beds. The black diamonds here are intelligent, cultured with a complex language and literature as of yet untranslatable and mostly psychic in nature. Their mathematics are supremely advanced and befuddle even the brainiest earth mathematicians. All life on Planet X is black and Crystalline.

We wandered Planet X for days, a smooth cool desert of obsidian jutting with mesas, arcs, crystalline formations of all manners, stopping at oases, creeks and tributaries for swigs of the powerful black water. It was a group walkabout. We walked in silence, breathing slow, in deep deep meditation, our collective psychic energies hallucinating shimmering black rainbow patterns across our brains.

I don't know how long we wandered and I don't believe it matters. We may have wandered forever, we may still be wandering there now as u read this, we may have never wandered, may be yet to wander, maybe it was a couple hours, I don't know.

But eventually we had to return back to the Rosa 2, who carried us back to our seaside village on earth.

Hakim and Maria split home with Lupe and Rosa, me and Khadija, Fatima and Madonna went on a walk.

The bright white sun was low slung and romantic, mildly eerie, the cacti and scrubby brush and rocks and whatnot cast cute lil blue shadows. Winds tickled us. The sea air danced against our skins.

Earth, Mexico. La Tierra. Rock, sand.

A rattlesnake rattled behind a nearby rock. Lifted its head and whispered, "Hola."

We returned its greeting.

He asked us for 50 pesos. I tapped my pockets: "no lo tengo."

"Chingaso…"

He slinked off.

We stomped the yard a lil mo came back inside.

Fatima and Madonna went to bed. We got stoned and watched a Marx Bros marathon on TV.

I was so stoned I felt like I was watching a live broadcast.

So stoned man. Hella high. Like wow, how did I get that high, I don't know.

Fell asleep on the couch. Woke up to Khadija tugging on me saying "Let's go to bed."

I said, "O.K."

Fausto stayed out there at Santa Sirena casino, still shooting dice, a man possessed, just like his pops.

65.

Khadija and I went on a date to the Santa Sirena Museo Del Arte. They had a small Frida Kahlo show, nice selection of works on loan. Their permanent collection had Rivera, O'Keefe, Bourgeois, Carrington, Izquierda, Julia Lopez, Diana Salazar, Ana Mendieta. An amazing collection.

The building was old, mision-esque, white arches, cobblestone courtyard with a fountain, long sunny big-windowed painting-lined hallways.

Marty and Malika were down visiting from the yay and were watching Fatima, Madonna and Fausto.

We hit a lil ristorante for dinner. She had tamales de peña and I had enchiladas de baca guey. We shared a bottle of 2012 Opus from Napa, a dark, dry tannic cab with curious notes of cherry, almost as if a splash of merlot fell in the tub in a happy accident. The enchiladas were banging too, saucy as fuck, rich, curious notes of chocolate, almost as if a splash of molé fell on the plate in a swaggy accident. We finished the meal off with espresso and some fire azz flan.

The ristorante had a giant hearth with a roaring fuego, huge exposed wood beams, cast iron candelabras. The whole experience was fire flames. What a fucking date. Wow. We were real pros at this.

We wandered thru the skreets of Santa Sirena, churches, taquerias, cantinas and other various dining halls, a public park here and there, low bridges over shallow creek beds, narrow calles cutting diagonally, curving in half circles around this or that historical statue, street vendors peddling tacos, tamales, elote, paletas, it was all muy classico. Lovebirds were out canoodling, families having a night on the town, wide-eyed turistas wandering drunk from lounge to lounge, grifters watching for the come up, hustlers and the like, eyes sharp for the next lick for the hitting, bulky brown laborers and lean loafers alike throwing their pay on the ground in dice games both literally and metaphorically, I thought I saw Fausto out there but I banished the thought from my mind. He was with Malika and Marty, ostensibly and he was certainly sharper than me, just like his mom. He could take care of himself and preferred to. We walked on, me thinking about my yung sun Fausto. Khadija was quiet too, kinda just surfing reality and letting me think to myself a bit, graciously, we walked thru agendas where borachos yodeled corridas out the pores of reefs of cervezerias, the steel strings and wheezing accordions, weeping canciones rancheros, peoples, birds, dogs and cats walking the placid streets in peace with their sad wise eyes.

We soaked in the scene, the stars twinkled above.

We hopped in the Jeep back to our cliffside/seaside house on the southern outskirts of town, rumbled along the dirt roads, roadrunners and iguanas darting out of our way in the deep magenta dusklight.

We made it back, kids were asleep. Marty and Malika were watching the only movie we owned, Dreyer's 1928 Passion de Jeanne d'Arc, loving it.

We sat and watched with them, ate popcorn and vanilla Swiss almond ice cream (lil vegan cheat day 4 Dij), drank red wine, smoked a doob. We hit our respective rooms and turned in early. We were headed up to Playa San Orfeo the next day to surf.

After some quiet, mellow coitus, Khadija said "Happy anniversary."

I didn't know it was our anniversary, but I didn't let on.

"Happy anniversary."

As far as ur boy's concerned, every day is the wedding, the honeymoon and the anniversary.

66.

I zipped on mee Yoka Yola in the zun. It was a zuper zunny day, zero cloudz in the zky, just zweet expanzive blu, felt like a yung Yamez Yoyce.

I was sitting at a lil picky nicky table on my lonely, barely wondering what to do next. No real plans, wants or desires to speak of.

I felt like an angel. Then I felt like a devil. Then I felt neutral. Then I went back to feeling like an angel but this time more muted, less rapturous. The brain operates in an oscillatory manner, I find.

The brain oscillates because it's made of particles that are made of particles that are made of particles that oscillate, quiver between this reality and that. At least that's my vague impressionistic view of things. Semantics hamper extra linguistic truths mane. The truth of the matter is that we both are and are not. That's how I feel, at least. And who am I?

U find urself reading this book, encountering its vague semblances of story and haphazardly rendered tableau of characters interacting in various settings and that's pretty much it. This is it, this is the book, are u enjoying it? Is it O.K.? Of course it is.

We're entering the third act, how do u feel? What's going on in ur life? U doing O.K.? U must be doing O.K. At the very least, u found the time to sit down a read a book, that's an applaudable feat. Relax, kick ur feet up, enjoy a beverage, look up at the sky. The sky is cool, it always looks good. The sky is the first supermodel. And the last.

Are u wondering what's going to happen next or are u just chilling out, enjoying the ride? I hope ur just enjoying the ride because I don't like the pressure of having to render interesting plot points for u. Don't seek too hard, u kno? It just stresses u out and that stresses me out. Look, I don't have any painstakingly crafted lessons for u. I'm of the school that lessons needn't be crafted, they occur regardless, which is to say I'm not of the school in any sense of the word. I went to a few schools and had a decent enuf in time in all of them but the best school is life, always was, always will be.

If u don't "get it" that's fine, u don't have to. What's there to get? Life's punchline is death and it occurs whether u get it or not. Act 3 finna be tight mane just wait and see, it's gona be a lot of poetic passages and all that novel navel gazery u've come to love in this delicious lil book so far.

O.K. leme see, what next?

I finished my soda pop, got up from the picnic table, stretched, yawned, the muted angelic vibes sort of evaporated and I felt regular again.

I walked around Santa Sirena on the solo dolo tip, people gazing, sun soaking.

I started levitating about a half foot off the ground. A wandering hound gazed at ur boy, his eyes glassy and remarkable.

He said: "Woof!"

And I said: "woof" right back at him.

I levitated a lil higher, I was now about a foot off the ground. An ol vieja waddled past, looked up and crossed herself saying: "¡Ay Dios Mio!"

I said: "Dios te bendiga mami."

She smiled, seemed relieved that whatever magic that was occurring seemed to be more angelic than demonic.

Satisfied, she went upon her way.

I ambled along.

What else, what else?

All of a sudden I was on a boat in the middle of the sea.

A giant squid popped his head out the water, gazed at ur boy with an eyeball the size of a dinner plate.

Squid said: "Ay!"

I was like "sup"

Squid was like "U got a cigarette?"

I was like "Naw fam, my fault."

Then I was at the Great Pyramids of Egypt gazing up at a big ass Pyramid.

What a sight, man.

Then I was on a horse galloping thru the Amazonian rainforest.

Man, ur boy cooking, this novel go hard, a true delight. This is a good book man, this book is at least as good as The Sound and the Fury by Billy Faulkner.

O.K., let's see, what else, what else?

Naw I think I'm done with this chapter, see u in the next one.

67.

Whew, glad that last chapter is over, it was not that great. Naw whatever, it was O.K.

So me and the missus were in Berlin with Afrooz and Medina and Khadija's gay bestie Jebediah. Jeb and Khadija hadn't seen each other in hella long and were in high spirits. Hella giddy. Fatima and Madonna were in Istanbul with Khadija's mom. Fausto was in Macau gambling. We were all linking up the next day somewhere in Bahrain me and wifey but wanted to check out the Berlin club scene first.

The homie Adél threw us on the list at some spot called The Vortex we walked over and skipped the line, ran into Adél on the the dance flo, she took us over to VIP gave us glasses of champagne with ecstasy sprankled in them. Mali and Violin were there and Violin's homie Theo, and The Dangler was there too and Adél's dude Hans from the band White White Animals and Adél's girls Hyun and Jeong were there too and some other German dude and his German girl who I guess Adél knew.

I fixed myself a cranberry vodka and lamped on the couch with Mali, Hans, Jeb, The Dangler and The Other Germans while the girls all danced with Theo. Theo was a tall gay dude from the islands, he danced like a big graceful swan, the ladies loved him.

Hans busted out some yay. We sniffed that.

I felt hella sparkly, the drugs was working. I took in the scene, it was hella dark with flashing colored lights, blacklight, disco balls, fog, oppressively loud techno. All in all it seemed very German. A strange culture. Theo, Violin and

Khadija came back asking if me and Mali wanted to dance. We politely declined but did sniff some of Theo's ketamine.

As the night wore on, I started to really like the music, I believe it was a decision made for me by the drugs. Stockholm Syndrome vibes in there, I felt like a captured Taliban warrior at a really really chill Gitmo. I almost felt like dancing but the Coke and Molly and ketamine combined were so strong I just stayed plastered on the couch feeling insanely, nervewrackingly euphoric. Mali seemed to be in a similar situation.

"U good bruh?" I shouted over at him.

"I'm hella high nigga!" He responded.

"Me too!"

We left around 6 in the morning and the party seemed like it was nowhere near over but we were tired and hungry and out of cocaine. We hit the kebab spot then retired to an apartment where we smoked hash and drank coffee and listened to David Bowie records. More my speed to be perfectly honest.

We cracked some red wine, listened to Bob Marley, Adél found some adderalls and vicodins I had a little of both.

At some point somebody told me that rando German wasn't a rando German at all but famous American Hollywood actor Eli Madera.

I was like "whoa."

No wonder the vibe had been so heady.

Adél and Hans set up a microphone and we all recorded freestyles over the Benjamins beat.

Mine was like:

ALLAH TRUTH
SWEET EXSTASY
TRUTH PEACE ALLAH

JAH JAH
U KNO HOW WE DO
TRUTH INFINITE
INFINITE JEST
JUST DO IT
THE POWER OF CHRIST COMPELS ME
L'CHAIM
SMOKE WEED
HAIL SATAN
ALI BUMBAYE
CIAO BELLA
TRIVELLINO
REAL NIGGA WASSUP
KNOWLEDGE WISDOM UNDERSTANDING
FORGIVE ME FOR I KNO NOT WHAT I DO
AND SAY
WHATS A YUNG MULATTO SOUL 2 DO
OM SHANTI OM
THERE IS NO TRUTH
U EITHER BUILD OR DESTROY
THE ONLY CONSTANT IS CHANGE
FLUX, PURE ENERGY
THE SINISTER ENERGIES OF EUROPE COL-
LAPSE AT THRONE OF MAMA AFRICA
THE WIZARDRY OF ALEXANDRIAN MATHE-
MATICS PREVAILS, IMMACULATE
THE GOLDEN SUN THE SILVER MOON AND
VICE VERSA
¡A GOZAR! ¡A BAILAR!
ET CETERA
CHANGO
YEMAYA

YEMAYA

We mixed and mastered the track right then and there sent it to the local radio station, they played it, it was a major hit, the royalty checks rolled in perpetua.

68.

"Fuck everything."

Riffzo was over, we were drinking beers and smoking weed on the deck.

"Everything sux."

"The world is weak."

"The world is utter trash."

"Complete and total garbage."

"Why bother."

"Life sux."

"No hope."

"No silver lining in the clouds."

"This world is shite brutha."

"What a world, am I right?"

"Pure garbage."

"Utter refuse."

"What's the use?"

"Useless."

"Fear, hatred!"

"Tyranny!"

"Fascist winds!"
"The vile swine of capitalism!"
"The violent hogs parading as protectors!"
"The hubris, the wild arrogance!"
"The lies!"
"Real eyes realize real lies!"
"The grizzly, blood soaked war machine!"
"The dead-eyed soldiers of terror!"
"The false prophecies!"
"The fraudulent democracies!"
"The greed!"
"Lust! Gluttony!"
"The rank stench of humanity!"
"Sadness!"
"We are pitiable creatures!"
"Deplorable, we!"
"Shameful!"
"O!"
"Hark!"
"Alas!"
"Alack!"
"Alee!"
"Woe!"
Wifey stepped outside with a plate of tacos she made.
"What are u losers up to?"
"Oh snap, tacos."
"Hell yea."

69.

"Om gon ganapatayeh namaha."

Bae was chanting at the crib.

"Free Palestine," I said, joining in for a bit o' the ol' call-n'-response.

"Om gon ganapatayeh namaha."

"Free Afghanistan."

"Om gon ganapatayeh namaha."

"Pedagogy as hypnosis."

"Om gon ganapatayeh namaha."

"Existence is hypnotic."

"Om gon ganapatayeh namaha."

"Black lives matter."

"Om gon ganapatayeh namaha."

"Peace to the soul and family of Tamir Rice."

"Om gon ganapatayeh namaha."

"Peace to the soul and family of Sandra Bland."

"Om gon ganapatayeh namaha."

"Trayvon, Oscar, Eric, Sean, Amadou."

"Om gon ganapatayeh namaha."

"Abolish prison."

"Om gon ganapatayeh namaha."

"Jah Rastafari."

"Om gon ganapatayeh namaha."

"CHANGO."

"Om gon ganapatayeh namaha."

"YEMAYA."

"Om gon ganapatayeh namaha."

"ALLAH."

"Allah."

Fatima was working on the blueprints for her latest work, a white gold hawk called the Guadalupe 2. It looked to be her most beautiful project yet. Madonna was providing the psychic energy via heavy meditation.

Khadija switched up to the Sarasvati chant. I joined in for a while then got bored smoked a doob, took a nap. Woke up and she was stroking my head chanting "Krishna, Krishna" in a whisper and Fatima and Madonna were taking a nap. Fausto was still out there shooting dice somewhere, winning.

I kizzed me wife, we made some love.

Allah hu Akbar.

She put on a Francoise Hardy record. She kept coming back to this one.

She made some tea while I laid on the sofa gazing out the window.

Fatima woke up, went back to her blueprints.

Me and Khadija had a sweet convo whilzt zippin tea:

"Existence is suffering."

"Suffering is nothing."

"Perpetual desire."

"Desire is nothing."

"Molecular delusion."

"Abandon desire."

"Abandon truth consciousness."

"Truth beyond truth."

"Beyond the veil, a world beyond language."

"A reality beyond reality."

"Truth, mighty."

She burned some incense put on some EDM. Marty and Malika strolled in from the other room, hella forgot they were still here.

I went on a walk.

The ocean was glittering, shimmering, iridescent, turquoise, violently happy.

I walked past an abandoned church some fools was squatting in, down a long dirt road to a cliff with steps carved into it leading down to a rock sheltered tide pool.

A rock slipped loose under my foot and I fell against the rock wall, my left hand brushed a cactus and my right arm scraped against some rocks and started bleeding.

I picked the needles out my left hand and continued climbing down to the tide pool, stripped naked, jumped in. The cold salt water stung my cuts but I felt washed, healed and rejuvenated. I laid out on a rock to dry out. The waves crashed and echoed in the little rocky bay. My arm and hand stung but the stinging sensation was strangely refreshing, made everything feel vivid and electrically real. Such a specific feeling I hadn't felt in a while, an earthly pain as the opposed to The Pain which was deep, cosmic, existential in nature.

That's what's up.

When the sun had finished drying ur boy I put my clothes back on and hiked on back.

Sat on the deck with a beer listening to the Thelonius Monk record tinkling in the living room.

Monk was a real Bodhisattva mane, his harmony game was skrong and skrange.

Looked at the sky. Life, mane. I wonder. Will it take me under?

70.

I was walking around the Lower East Side high off a weed brownie and some speed, chiefin a loosie, it was nice and sunny out. I had on a throwback Jabbar Bucks jersey, I was feelin myself.

Walked over to the cheap Indian joint where all the cab drivers eat lunch, copped a samosa and some mango juice. I wasn't hungry, I just wanted something to do.

Ran into Critter and Fearless we built as we walked over to the corner where Hi-Five, White Dog and Arkady said link with them. El Indio slid up on us: "Peace Allah" we responded in kind, chopped it up on the topic of various knowledges and books, as we walked.

Over at the specified corner we all ran into Hi-5, W Dog, and Arky. El Indio peaced. We all walked mobbishly over to an Italian spot got some pastas and pizzas and coffees and such.

I went to the bathroom with Hi-5 sniffed some dope then I came back and sleepily ate some pasta.

Critter and Fearless cut out.

We walked over to Misty Dolphin's got beers, posted up there a while. Smiley was bartending and hooked it up. Sue was working the door but it was slow so he was sitting drinking with us mostly.

White Cat slid up. White Cat is Pinoy but his complexion is pretty white, which I guess is why, like, u kno, hence, the name.

Dart Quickly passed by I walked outside to say what up. He had just made a couple mil on a distro deal for a clothing company he had started. He was feeling relaxed. Last time I saw him he was stressed out talking about "I might need to sell one of the mansions." I had told him that was nonsense and now we were having a laff about that. The homie Melissa walked by I hadn't seen her in hella long she was on her way to bartend at The Red Accordion, Dart said peace and cut, I convinced Melissa to come in a have a shot of whiskey with us before she went on her way. She told us swing by The Accordion later we were like O.K.

I got sick and threw up a bit in the bathroom. Hi-Five gave me another bag of dope and an adderall. I had been off dope for a while and wasn't quite used to mixing it with other drugs and drink like I used to but after throwing up and drugging a bit more I was in a decent feeling. I nursed a beer for an hour, maybe two. We moved over to The Accordion and I had another two hour beer. It was late by then but I decided to cop a beer at the bodega and walk over the bridge to Brooklyn. I was a bit chilly in my jersey but feeling good and not trippin off it, sipping at my beer, I hadn't gone but like 3 blocks when a copper jumped from behind a corner and hemmed ur boy up. I had some old warrant so I had to spend the night in the clinko. Luckily I had finished my dope or else they'd have found that and I'd be in some deeper shit.

This particular pig was a white Puerto Rican, name tag said Ortiz. He had a Captain America tattoo, a real loser. His partner was a sweet faced black Dominican chick, name tag said Abreu. She had kind eyes, I wondered why she would decide to be a cop. They cuffed me, drove me to the precinct, fingerprinted me. Ortiz was nice enough too actually, just doing his job I guess. So was Eichmann tho.

They drove me down to the tombs or the catacombs or whatever they be calling central bookings lately, and the all too familiar long tedious bureaucratic chain gang ensued with the mugshots and everything before I ended up in a cold ass cell with like 20 dudes. All the inmates were black or "Spanish" as they say in New York and most of the cops were white except for the two that had brought me in (now gone) and an old black cop by the door.

Then a thick brown black lady cop brought out the shitty lil stale sandwiches and milk, I was like no thanks.

I poured some sink water in my hand and splashed it in my mouth but the sink looked dirty and was right next to the filthy toilet so I didn't take another drink. Actually almost threw up right there but held back figuring the smell would linger all night and make me unpopular.

I closed my eyes and meditated as I came off all the drugs. I faintly heard other dudes tell jail stories and prison stories and drug dealing stories, knock knock jokes, some knowledge, some science, some darts, some shadowboxing, chess boxing, lyrical origami, some lessons, some jokes and bullshit. It's interesting enough when ur in the mood but it all blends together when ur not, just like anything else. I was cold but I didn't shiver.

I had a bad headache and was thirsty and hungry and a little nauseous but at least I wasn't going to prison like some of these dudes. That very thought nearly cured my headache.

At a certain point I fell asleep sitting up. Morning came and they took us upstairs and we waited for the lawyers to call our names and talk to us thru the lil windows.

"Denzel Washington."

Everybody looked up.

It wasn't Denzel. Another dude. Same name.

They called my name, the lawyer was like "don't trip" I was like "I know"

I waited a bit longer was led into the court room, waited some more, judge talked at me, told me to bounce, I did.

I went outside and threw up on the sidewalk. Copped 4 tylenols and a Poland Spring at the bodega and housed those in 5 seconds flat. Got another Poland Spring and housed that. Walked to a Chinese spot drank like 5 more glasses of water and a pot of tea then had some chicken wings and a Tsing Tao, took the train to BK, kissed my wife and daughters (Faustino still out Allah knows where), slept all day at the church attic pad while wifey sewed a rug for Roxana on her Turkish loom and Fatima worked on her blueprints.

I woke up in the early evening and it started to rain. We made tea and sipped it listening to Sketches of Spain, one of my favorites.

71.

We were in a stretch limo headed to a wedding in Jersey. Khadija's girl Yesenia was marrying a Chinese dude named Chin at some nice lil spot on the Hudson. We sniffed cocaine and drank champagne in the limo. Sinu and Silverstein were with us. Roxana and Jermaine were watching Fatima.

We got to the spot pretty buzzed. The ceremony was brief, the dinner was delicious. Me and Silverstein had the steak, Sinu and wifey had the chicken.

The wedding band had a saxophonist who looked like an aging, strung out Kenny G. Maybe it was Kenny G, I hadn't been keeping track of where that dude had been lately. Kenny was blowing hard tonite. The band played all the wedding hits. U know the ones, it's too boring a task for me rite nao 2 recount them here.

"Heaven is where u will be when u are O.K. right where u are," I whispered in my wife's ear.

"That's sweet."

"It's Sun Ra."

"Are u in Heaven?"

"Usually. Like probably almost always."

"I meant now."

"Oh now? Yeah, hell yeah, this wedding is tight."

"Ur tight."

"UR tight!"

Ur boy was drunk. Wifey was kinda drunk too, a rare occasion. We were both feeling feisty. I almost got into a fight, don't quite remember over what. Silverstein broke it up and we went to go sniff some yayo in the elegant washroom.

"U gota chill mane, Yesenia's fam don't play."

"I don't even remember how that started bruh I'm toe up."

"It's all good mane I think I handled it."

"Ay bruh it's all love mane I'm good if they good and if they wana scrap I'll scrap."

"Naw, naw chill chill b."

"O.K."

We ended up in Windmill Gardens in Brooklyn, drinking and sniffing more yola, Silverstein had too much of the stuff had to sell it off sometimes. His white goon friend was there, kept talking about how he had to "suplex" a guy and throw him out a second story window the other day. I was all ears.

There was a couple other people there, I don't remember their names I was too fucked up.

At a certain point I sneezed a decent amount of a coke off the mirror like in that Woody Allen movie.

"Oh shit, my bad, that was hella weak of me, I feel like Woody Allen."

"Isn't that nigga like a rapist?"

"He's definitely an abuser of some stripe."

We bullshitted for another couple hours, Khadija fell asleep on a couch. We drank whiskey, listened to Migos.

At some late hour we bid adieu.

The next day we flew out to Virginia for another wedding, the homie Dave Leong was marrying his pink toe Martha. It was an extravagant barn wedding. I got toe up on whiskey but Khadija held it down and kicked it with Fatima and Madonna since we didn't have a babysitter.

We stayed at the Greenbrier. The wallpaper was wild floral. Earth, Wind and Fire played. I won a couple grand at the casino, bought some Polo gear for myself, a makeup bag for wifey, little sun hats for Fatima and Madonna, nothing for Fausto, he was only interested in gambling, in fact he was playing dice at some other casino across town.

We flew to Napa for a vineyard wedding. Khadija's girl Scrappy and her dude Ashley. It was a sweet lil ceremony, wild hot, everybody sweating and fanning themselves with little wicker fans that had been placed under each seat. Fatima and Madonna had stayed in New York with Roxana and Jermaine, who were flying out to meet us the next day in Santa Sirena.

Fausto was back in Macau, I think.

At dinner we were seated next to Scrappy's brother Gaspar and his wife Yasmin, they gave us some strong ass weed candies and we eventually wandered off to a little gazebo with them and smoked a doob while they pontificated on the Annunaki, the ancient gods of Mesopotamia, whom they claimed were cosmic beings from another galaxy that brought human consciousness to earth, something along those lines. They were very rehearsed and eloquent on the subject, tag-teaming and finishing each other's sentences, u could tell they'd had many a late night discussion on the subject, they recommended some literature to us. Khadija promised to look into it, but most of the authors sounded too Western so we forgot them.

We got wine drunk, I even danced a tiny bit. I kept my sunglasses on thru the nite.

Next morning we cut to Santa Sirena, showed up at the crib an hour before Fatima, Madonna, Roxana and Jermaine showed up, were stepping out the shower when they knocked. We let them in, got some clothes and went to get breakfast at this lil seaside restaurant, came back and we all snoozed around all day.

In the late afternoon, we all walked over to a large pen where a neighbor kept two majestic deer and we fed them some carrots, patted their soft heads as they wiggled their wet noses at us. Fatima lightly touched the male's antlers but then he got skittish and trotted out of reach.

We walked over to an abandoned cliffside church and watched the sunset, deep red pink and purple, and, like the deer, quite majestic. It was all one majesty, the deer, the sea, the sun, the purple mountains, the vineyards, gazebos, barns, hotels, casinos, skyscrapers, jails, prisons, churches, temples, a bittersweet symphony mane, that's life, tryna make ends meet tryna make some money then u die, the cosmic rainbow man, the majesty, Purple Mountain Majesty, the sad sick majesty, the sad beautiful majesty, the tragic majesty, the magic tragedy, the cold echoing emptiness of space, the boiling hot stars, the other matter floating around, the earth in its simple sad majesty, the human animals scrambling across land and churning violent sea, zooming into the air, longing, forever longing, it was all the same majesty bruh, the same sad beautiful majesty mami, the majesty papo, the Majestic Eagles in flight, the Majestic Falcons & Hawks, the cosmic flying carpet, the Majestic Dragons of the mind the majestic crawling vines and lil ivies of the soul, all the same majesty, the bubbling useless chatter of human consciousness, the Annunaki blazing thru the universe and crashing into a lonely, happenstantial muds of Mesopotamia, who would have thunk, mane, we here thunk this majesty up and it was served up to us on its own majestic platter, what a strange trip to be alive, such majesty.

72.

I was at the crib studying the daily fluctuations of the pmeso-to-dollar exchange rate, I had a little currency trading racket giving me some pocket money for the time being.

Khadija, Fatima, Madonna, Roxana and Jermaine came back from a walk. I shut my ancient laptop computer, drank an Indio with Jermaine on the deck.

Fausto was in Costa Rica last I heard.

Maestro, Maria, Lupe and Rosa came thru. Lupe and Rosa ran off with Fatima to work on Guadalupe 2. Khadija made some margaritas and we all chilled on the deck.

Marty, Malika, Munda, Ali Ala and his daughter Sabrina showed up. Fuck I had forgot they were coming. Sabrina was Fatima's age but they rarely saw each other cause she mostly stayed in Paris with her mom. We hollered for Fatima and she came running in, took Sabrina's hand and dragged her over to her lil workshop with Lupe and Rosa, set her to work on the Guadalupe 2: The White Gold Hawk.

We adults drank our little margaritas and chit chatted. Munda didn't drink, she was off the stuff.

"How u been Munda, haven't see u in hella long," I asked her.

"Same old."

"How's dude?"

"Broke up with him."

"Sorry to hear that."

"Naw he was terrible."

"What about homeboy from before with the-"

"We're texting again."

"I like that dude."

"He's O.K."

"How's the jewelry?"

"Working on a commission right now."

"Yeah?"

"Rosary for the principal of Colegio de Santa Marta Del Dolor."

"Tight."

"The beads are made from the bones of her grandmother."

"Wow."

"It's painstaking work, a lot of prayer involved."

"I would imagine."

We all lamped on the deck. It was a full house, I felt like Bob Saget.

We listened to Joaquin Rodrigo.

Maestro Hakim Karim Allah kicked a freestyle:

Slowly beginning to feel the weight
All my burdens becoming so great
But yet I don't complain
For the heavy load of my assignment
Like the hull of a weary train
Steaming across this age old prairie
So vast, so mighty, in steel,
Obediently I tote the heavy load
Sustained by a determined wheel
Though growing tired, with eyes of age
But refusing to abandon my toil
For my working day shan't be over
Until my return to the soil
But somewhere in the yonder of unused time
I'll continue to tote this heavy load
For the burden I bear is mine.

A skrong poem. One of the best I'd ever heard. We all clapped.

The ocean waves down the hill hissed and shushed and sighed emphatically.

Threw on some Joaquin Rodrigo and some Mongo Santamaria on after that, drank, wuz merry.

Somebody asked me if I had ever read James Joyce, I was like yea he's tight.

Writing a book is hard mane it takes hella long just sitting there writing all those words. What the fuck. Props to anybody who even gets published, convince somebody to chop down a few trees for ur tired ass. Who cares about what any single solitary creature has to say that much that it's worth hella trees dying? I don't know man on the other hand it's hella trees out there what's a few if it means something warm to curl up to at night? That's what a fire is for I guess. But even a fire gets boring sometimes, right? Plus u can farm trees right? Iono mane, I'm no geographical planner type.

Way I see it, probably best to work on telepathy, faith, communalized intelligence, love, peace, breathing, the exercise of the fragile, mortal human muscles.

M.H.K.A., Maria, Lupe and Rosa cut out.

Munda, Malika, Marty, Ali Ala and Sabrina stayed over. Sabrina stayed in Fatima and Madonna's room, they worked on the Guadalupe blueprints, every now and then Malika or Khadija or Munda would go in and check on them.

We continued to chop it up. We didn't drink that much. Munda's soberness was contagious and actually quite refreshing.

It was a fun convo mane, hella real, so real it seems stupid to transcribe it here.

The day passed and pretty soon we found ourselves in Chapter 73.

73.

The next day, Fatima and Sabrina woke up early, Malika and Munda tended to them while Me and Khadija slept in.

Marty and Ali Ala sat on the deck looking at the beach sippin cafe correcto then went down to the playa with the girls.

Me and the wife buns-ed around, slept a bit more, woke up, had some coffee, we all hit the beach, kicked it there most of the day, sat there looking at the ocean waves, the ceaseless ocean waves, ancient, older than man, the mama that Orisha Yemaya, oceanic earth, I am ur native son KOOL ALLAH DADA MOHAMMAD X CHANGO JAH RASTA OM OOM BOOM BUMBAYE BONG BONG CONGA CONGA CHANGO BAM BAM BARAKA SHAKA OOGA CHAKA BEMBE ALLAH JAH CHANGO.

Bruh, let me tell u it was a sweet day.

Sun shining, errythang.

Mellow, the faintest breeze.

I had brought some Chekov to the beach pretended to read it for like 5 minutes then went swimming, fell asleep on the towel.

Truth, beauty, understanding.

The day was beautiful, it bears repeating.

Bruh, I was high at that beach, I won't lie. I had a lil cookie earlier, Ali Ala had brought down a lil ice box o beers, the waves were insistent and beautiful, the sun a perfect yellow, the sky a perfect blue, I was ziplining thru existence.

We walked on back up the hill, Marty made some tacos, Malika made margaritas.

Listened to Bob James for a second then switched it to Sun Ship played that joint a couple times in a row, smoked weed, drank beers, bullshat. Warriors beat the Spurs on TV, go Warriors.

I always dug San Anto' tho. Remember the Alamo, feel me? I used to walk those beautiful skreets slanging plasma, the plasma of the soul, it transfused with the earth, wrought delicate sculptures of light and flesh, beckoning and screaming in delight, ghostly visages, the twisting elm, the sacred holly vines, the leafy flower blossoms of harmony and sweet white hot terror and joy and sorrow, the jingling piano keys o' death the truest most horrible, beautiful infinite concepts, theological, of the spirit, enduring, a flapping sail on an azure sea of adventure, a ganglion of lightnings for our wonder, o theez pitiful &' useless wurds, English is a trick! English is a sappy poison from the branch of imperialism! How do we rid ourselves of it? Doth I protest and what not, feel me?

Day turned to nite again, we hit the lil bazaar the next day it was both Marty and Karim-Hakim Hakim Karim Allah's bday, coincidentally. I copped Marty a lil Dia de los Muertos type Calaveras style clay skull craneo type thang w a Chargers helmet painted on it and I copped Hakim-Karim another lil D. De la M. Cally-V Skullz but this 1 had a raiders helmet painted on it. Both highly wavy finds.

We ate at an large expansive seaside taqueria. There was a couple singing old Mexican tunes, dude had a vintage like late 70's Rhodes electric keyboard with the reverb cranked it added an ethereal quality to the music.

We took shots of some old smooth tequila with the singers and the barkeep I literally don't remember any of their names I learned them all when I was black out drunk. The ladies headed back to the house and me and Hakim Karim and Marty and Ali Ala stayed back throwing back Indios.

"Literature is, at its most base, espionage," said Ali Ala.

"No doubt."

Hakim/Karim produced a white dove from one sleeve and a pair of dice from the other.

We all played dice for a while, the barkeep won. Ali Ala came up, I broke even. Marty lost a lot, the singers lost a lot, Hakim broke even.

The sun got hella hot and intense and then set, leaving the sky a deep mellow red before turning blue.

We hit the house for mas cafe correcto, played some Don Cherry on the record player, then Marty dug thru the crate and dusted off one I hadn't heard in a while a record by the Torala Orchestra of Algiers. They played some hyper real chamber music plucked from all around the Mediterranean and North Africa. They had this one Arab number called YA BAY! ("Alas!") a sad lyrical joint about love lost but the music was hella jubilant, a real slapper. Sounded like they were saying "Ya boy! Ya boy! Ya boy! Ya boy!" And in way they were, they were telling ur boy's story. The story of every boy and girl on earth, love, disappointment, life goes on, alas, etc.

Khadija made some sweet hibiscus tea and we spiked it with Tequila. She aux cord DJ-ed some house music on her phone. The Belleville 3 outa Detroit and than this Hungarian kid, Gergely Szilveszter Horváth, real melancholy stuff with some beautiful crisp ass drum tones, then some DJ Nate da Trak Genious then back to Belleville 3, DJ Rolando, Rhythm is Rhythim, etc., then she got into a lot more esoteric techno shit that went beyond the depth of my knowledge on the subject, she was an exquisite house DJ.

It got colder and crisper. The nite roared on, muted dark blak blu. Yes.

74.

We were all posted at the crib getting lit watching Scarface (me, wifey, Maestro Hakim Karim Karim Hakim Allah, Maria, Marty, Malika, Munda, Ali Ala, Roxana, Jermaine) when Fatima came running in tailed by Madonna, Lupe, Rosa and Sabrina. They had The Guadalupe 2: White Gold Hawk in tow, fully operational and shined up, sparkling new.

"¡Se acabo!"

"Wow!"

We took it on a test drive, whipped on over to NYC, me and Khadija asked to be dropped off over in TraBeKo (Trapezoid Below Kola Nut Circle), said peace to the squad, link with y'all later, and walked over to a fancy lil Post-French ristorante called Évènt.

The wine was a 1777 Shiraz, $777 bux.

Course one was a cube of smoke.

Course two was two leaves from an oak tree dipped in black ink.

Course three was two tiny beakers of hot pink milk, tasted sweet, carbonated.

Course four was six small white pebbles.

Course five was a living black widow spider that walked off the plate back into the kitchen and complained that there was no fly in his soup.

Course six was four tiny dabs of very spicy mustard.

Course seven was two tiny diamonds.

Desert was chocolate ice cream.

The meal cost $7,000 dollars, paired with the wine, it came to $7,777.

I tipped $2,222, I believe that's customary.

We took a cab over to the Imperialist State Building, went up top, looked out over New Golgotha. The observation deck was completely abandoned except for us.

"We had one of our weddings here, right?"

"Yes."

"Crazy."

"It's our anniversary."

"Ya tu sabe mami."

We smooched.

Lupe, the White Gold Hawk flew by, whole squad up in there, we hopped aboard.

"How was y'all's lil date?" Asked Jermaine.

"Deserved," replied Khadija.

"How u been Fatima?" I asked.

"Good," she said, focused on her piloting.

"She's a great pilot," Munda told me.

"Yeah, I know. How you, Madonna?"

"Chillin."

"Thaswasup."

Malika interjected: "Madonna, Lupe, Rosa and Sabrina are an able-bodied crew."

"But of course," I zed.

We swooped o'er the skreets o' Nueva Golgothita, casting shadows o'er the mumbling, bedraggled citizenry. The lites was lit and the automobiles rattled around like pinballs, El Gran Manzana.

We hit the moon, Shiraz, The Pain, Planet X, all the usual stops. We went about our lil businesses, dropped off Roxana and Jermaine, swung over to Sunset City dropped off Malika, Marty, Ali Ala and Sabrina, swung over to Oak Town, dropped Munda off at her new spot right off Landish Lake. She didn't want to invite us in.

"Next time. It's a mess."

"No doubt."

And then we flapped on back down to Santa Sirena, dropped off Maria, Maestro, Lupe and Rosa, then finally landed at the cribbo. Long day.

The Lupe 2 had flown like a dream, I beamed with pride for my lil girls. Everything they crafted was pure perfect beauty.

Fatima and Madonna yawned off to zleep.

Wifey boiled up some tea and we sipped on that, chiefin reefer, listening to Sade.

We did our lil thang, got to bed. The nite passed. Fausto out there in the world, dice hand still hot.

75.

I was out on the deck at the crib in Santa Sirena reading Infinite Jest, occasionally looking up at the rolling oceanic vista, sippin on a coffee, smoking a rare cig.

Fatima walked out on to the deck handed me Aime Cesaire's Discourse on Colonialism, I took the hint, put down I.J. and picked up D.O.C.

Opened at random to some fire barz:

Therefore, comrade, u will hold as enemies— loftily, lucidly, consistently— not only the sadistic governors and greedy bankers, not only prefects who torture and colonists who flog, not only corrupt, check-licking politicians and subservient judges, but likewise and for the same reason, venomous journalists, goitrous academics wreathed in dollars and stupidity, ethnographers who go in for metaphysics, presumptuous Belgian theologians, chattering intellectuals born stinking out of the thigh of Nietzsche, the paternalists, the embracers, the corrupters, the back-slappers, the lovers of exoticism, the dividers, the agrarian sociologists, the hoodwinkers, the hoaxers, the hot-air artists, the humbugs and in general, all those who, performing their functions in the sordid division of labor for the defense of Western Bourgeois Society, try in diverse ways and by infamous diversions to split up the forces of Progress— even if it means denying the very possibility of Progress— all of them tools of capitalism, all of them, openly or secretly, supporters of plundering colonialism, all of them responsible, all hateful, all slave-traders, all henceforth answerable for the violence of revolutionary action.

Phew, Cesaire was a real one. I personally felt he didn't have to shit on metaphysics but I knew I had to let dude cook, he was next level.

No sooner had I looked up than Madonna had brought me another book: Race, Women & Class by Angela Davis, I flipped that open and found some more fuego:

Black women had been more than willing to contribute clear powers of observation and judgement toward the creation of a multiracial movement for women's political rights but at every turn, they were betrayed, spurned and rejected by the leaders of the lily-white woman suffrage movement… Black women were simply expendable entities when it came time to woo Southern support with a white complexion.

I looked up and Fatima had brought me another book, a small white paperback I had never seen, didn't know where it came from, it read in plain text on the cover:

THE VOICE OF SILENCE

Being Extracts from

The

Book of the Golden Precepts

I flipped thru, THE SEVEN PORTALS, THE TWO PATHS, oh word it was a lil Buddhist book, tight:

Be humble, if thou would'st attain to Wisdom.

Be humbler still, when Wisdom thou hast mastered.

Be like the Ocean which receives all streams and rivers. The Ocean's mighty calm remains unmoved; it feels them not.

Restrain by thy Divine thy lower Self.

Restrain by the Eternal the Divine.

Aye, great is he, who is the slayer of desire.

Still greater he, in whom the Self Divine has slain the very knowledge of desire.

Guard thou the lowest lest it soil the higher.

The way to final freedom is within thy SELF.
That way begins and ends outside of Self.
Wow, yeah. Truly trippy stuff. Very wavy, very groovy.
"Y'all some brilliant professor babies."
Lo dos junto: "Ya tu sabe, papi."

76.

"Let me look at the waves in ur hair."
"What?"
"Nothing, u wana go to the beach?"
"O.K."
We went to the beach.

Khadija, Fatima and Madonna gamboled in the tide pools collecting cockles, mussels, etc. and I swam thru the ocean proper, over to a jutting rock and back, then laid out on a towel in the sand, soaking up the sun's dry heat.

A calico cat walked up to me, nudged her head under my hand, purring, cajoling ur boy into petting a yung cuddie, I complied.

We vibed, me and the calico, she was on the same wavelength as urz tru, thoughts paisley, slinking, sleepy, reticulate. Our minds webbed together in the sun soaked sky, reality splayed out blue and cloudy white in front of us, heaving, the ceaseless shushing ocean waves. I fell asleep as the lil feline curled itself up under my arm.

When I woke up, the cat had run off. Wife and child were ambling up with a bucket o' mussels and whatnot. We climbed the hill back up to the house and wifey cooked up the mussels in a garlic white wine sauce. Crack! Almost fell out my chair, that girl could cook.

After dinner I laid pon de couch, gazing at my wife, looking at the waves in her hair and whatnot, admiring her arabesque beauty, almond eyes and all that, full lips, the swell of the bosom, the curvatures, the smooth skin. I had really lucked out.

Our daughters was at the table, drawing up the blueprints to they next lil project, tentatively entitled The Beautiful Everything. It was unclear from the blueprints exactly what The Beautiful Everything was but it looked fractal in nature, prismatic, quantum, many splendored. Very penultimate, very be all end all. They might be ready to retire after this one. This one might be the one to have us all set, legs kicked up for the rest of our natural living perpetuity. I had nothing but the utmost hope, nay confidence, that this was the ultimate just of the strength of these early blueprints.

I burned a doob, threw on some Sly and the Family Stone and drifted off into an early sleep, woke up at around 2 in the morn. Nobody was up.

I walked down the hill in the black black blue nite, smoking a bogue, sat down on a round, surf-smoothed rock on the beach and stared into the deep black black blue waves reflecting the moon's eerie white blue light and the sparkling milky guey. What a scene. The waves mane, they don't stop, ceaseless mane, endless, no end, no cease: sssshhhh! sssshhhh! Ancient waves, timeless, ego-less salt water, insistent, declarative of nothing more nor less than its simple existence: sssshhhh! Sssshhhh! SSSSHHHH!

I climbed back up the hill and in front of the house came across a wild eyed coyote, he let out an eerie ethereal yelp. We stood transfixed, still, staring each other down.

He took his front right paw and moved it slowly to his hind quarters, pulled out his wallet and said:

"Here, take it, don't hurt me."

I said: "No, no, fear not, my coyote brother, I do not wish to hunt u for ur pelt."

"Phew!"

He wiped his forehead.

"Got a cigarette?"

I did.

We steamed bogies in the dark nite breeze then scampered off in our respective directions.

Went inside, climbed in bed, passed out. Another day accomplished, checked off the list of days to be lived.

77.

I was at Duggy Black's trap house in 77 Mile, up over Detroit way, I was on some business. Hi Five was there too, we were getting high off yay and diesel cut together. I hadn't messed with the stuff since the last time Hi Five had it, but he's a fun dude to do drugs with so I partook.

DuPont and White Marcus were there too we were in the kitchen, oven on and open. There was a shooter asleep on the couch in the living room with a nine peaking out the top of his pants (pause).

We were listening to Dej Loaf.

I was high as fuck listening to Hi Five rant about whatever popped into his head: Brian De Palma, Karl Marx, serial killers, Chinese Food, New York City Cops, Al Pacino, pizza, Naked Lunch, our homie Don Nixo, Royce Da 5'9, British radio, the history of salt, Nietzsche, Guy Debord, Knicks vs. Pacers NBA finals from whatever year that was hella long ago, how fun it felt to be on drugs, how much drugs sucked when they wore off, describing various near death experiences, some African movie called Touki Bouki, Peaky Blinders, Dizee Rascal, Margaret Cho, Quentin Tarantino, sushi…

White Marcus interjected: "I want some sushi."

Hi Five said: "Yeah me too."

Duggy said: "Me too."

Me too

DuPont too.

We climbed in the car, me, Hi Five, Duggy, Marcus, DuPont. The shooter stayed sleeping on the couch. No matter, Duggy, Marcus and DuPont were all strapped anyway.

White Marcus drove. It was Duggy's car but he was stoned and drunk and didn't feel like driving.

We listened to some Darq E Freaker on the way over to the sushi spot downtown.

It was like a full blown blizzard. Nobody was outside. The streets were empty, covered in snow.

For whatever reason, the sushi spot was open. It seemed miraculous to me.

We sat down, started blowing drugs off the table, handed a stack of hundos to the waiter and told him keep the sushi coming, whatever the sushi chef wanted to make was fine and bring a bunch of hot sake. He was like "bet" and we kicked it there for a few hours, White Dog slid thru, it was lit. Hi Five pontificated about more topics: The Sicilian Mafia's connection to the Vatican, the man-made scarcity of diamonds, value relative to cost as general concepts, some Indian mathematician I forget the name of now, the poetry of Rumi, Royce Da 5'9 again, Eminem, D12, Guilty Simpson, The White Stripes, Jim Jarmusch, The RZA, Kirosawa, Bruce Lee, Nacho Picasso, Al Pacino again, etc., etc. We threw them an extra rack at the end before cutting over to Coneys for chili cheese fries and then to a stash house in an undisclosed location. The stash, was more comfortable than the trap house, had central heating and big flat screen with hella DVDs, we put on Belly and Duggy called over some folks, it lightweight turned into a party. We all got fucked up on whiskey, smoked out of a bong and watched Aquateen Hunger Force while listening to MF Doom. Weird party. Me and Hi Five continued to speedball, he talked about Renoir the painter and Renoir the director, he talked about the French New Wave movement, he talked about Bertoldt Brecht ("what a clown") and Cornel West ("weirdly slept on"), he talked about Japanese woodblock printing, Van Gogh, Vermeer, the Dutch Masters, tales of getting his ass beat, the price of various organic foods, his vitamin regiment, how "filibuster" is a funny word, also "gubernatorial," the brutal, bloodsoaked mythical nature of American Democracy, the beat poets, Mexican food in San Francisco, Mexican food in Texas, Mexican food in the Midwest, Mexican food in New York, gas prices, 5 percenters, Al Qaeda, the night turned to dawn.

I caught a flying carpet over to Chicago, City of Wind. It was my great uncle Rogelio's 100 birthday, I stopped by his crib, he was carving a sculpture of his own head into a massive block of ebony on the freezing cold front porch in his wife beater, stopping to take swigs of ron oscuro.

"Feliz cumple tio."

"Gracia sobrinito, toma."

He handed me the bottle of rum I took a swig, walked thru the house said what up to the famalam, posted on the couch next to my primo Deon, chopped it up.

My great aunt Amalia had to run out and get Rogelio, "¡Acabalo ma' tarde, moriré de frio!" or somethin.

He moved the sculpture indoors and continued carving. Antonio Machin was playing.

I got drunk on rum, stepped outside to burn a blunt with Deon, he kicked me some codeine pills. Went back in, smashed on some picadillo and cut.

Caught the last magic carpet outa town, made it home in time for dinner, Macarooni Irooni. Bangin'.

Watched a Kirostami with the wife, sipped on an India Pale Ale that had been sitting in the fridge from when Marty had copped them. Smoked some tree. Fatima and Madonna fell asleep. Listened to some Leadbelly. Had some tequila. Burned poco mas, cuddled, bunsed, slept.

That was Chapter 77. Anyway, here's Chapter 78:

78.

Spent the morning listening to Jimi and watching Ravens bone in the sky.

Two nightingales landed on the dining room table and started nibbling at a plate of cannabis cookies.

They were gettin' high.

Bird one said to bird two: "Whoa…"

Bird two: "I know, right?"

Bird one: "It's crazy, like… we can fly."

Bird two: "I know I was just trippin off that too."

Bird one: (looks at wings)

Bird two: (looks at wings)

Both birds: "Whoa…"

Jimi Hendrix is a masterful player of the electrical guitar. I don't think anyone has come close to what he did in terms of soul and invention.

I went down to the strip and copped some more tree, came back, cooked up some cannaboid coconut oil and made platanos from the leftover plantains. The were half ripe so I did like a half tostone, half maduro recipe, half crispy, half juicy, the slight smash of the brown paper bag, seasoned with lemon, salt and sugar. Bruh, it was crack.

Zoomed on thru the day as per such.

Decided to write a letter to my pops, I hadn't seen him in a minute:

Sup papa,

Ain't seen u in a minute. Hope ur good.

Peace Allah Kinetic, Jah Rasta, CHANGO.

Ur sun,

X

Handed that off to a passing falcon, he swooped northward.

Wrote a letter to my mama:

Hola Mama,

Hope ur good, don't work too hard. Much love.

Ur sun.

Passed that off to a passing hawk. Wrote a letter to my dear sister Munda, we hadn't talked in a while:

Munda,

Love u always, no matter what.

Luh,

Bruh bruh

Passed that off to a passing dove. Wrote a letter to my other sister, Jamaica, she lived up in The Northern Woods, I hadn't visited in a long while:

Sis,

Ain't talked in a while my bad. I'm good tho. Hope ur good too. Much love. See u soon.

X

Passed that off to a passing raven.

Took a nap.

Wife & child came back from a walk.

I made steaks, pan fried potatoes and tomato avocado salad.

The sun brilliated then set.

We slept.

I dreamed of an empty city on a starless nite.

I awoke to a sleepy fishing village on a starry nite. The moon was full. Fatima was crying from a bad dream, Madonna waking up too, rubbing her eyes, starting to whine too. Fausto out gambling somewhere.

I took the girls out to the front deck and we looked up into the sky. The moon. Wow.

79.

I was in a Toyota Sienna, the rolling cacophonies of hypnotisms, the anarchy of magicks: Oakland parading past the windows, Lauryn Hill on the radio, it started to rain. I had nowhere to go for a couple hours, stoned, killin time, stopped at a red lite, on San Pablo and 30 something, lit a cig, threw on a OJ the Juiceman mixtape, zipped on, cracked the window, droplets of rain tickling the side of my neck and face, stopped at Black Summer got a coffee sat there drinking it looking out at the rain listening to Death sing Freakin Out, hopped back in the whipper, hit the trap house, then the stash house then the crash house, flipped on the telly, wrestled with Jimmy, watched Groundhog Day starring Bill Murray, then watched Ghostbusters one and two, the whole time chainsmoking swishers of OG kush, threw on some Lil B, watched M.A.S.H., played Candy Crush on my phone, flipped thru the autobiography of Thelonius Monk, listened to Monk: Alone in San Francisco, hopped in the Sebring, drove over to SF, drove around, got out in North Beach for an espresso, wandered around, hit City Lights, breezed thru a collection of Lorca poems, hopped back in the whipper hit Stow Lake, fed the ducks out of a bag of popcorn I had copped, walked over to the bison, said what up, walked over to the windmill, then the ocean, watched the sunset, drove back to the crash pad, watched Holy Mountain, read the Koran, flipped thru Octopus by Claire Sterling, flipped thru The Evil of the Day by Thomas Sterling, went out bombing with some neon orange spray paint I had found at the trap house, I hit an underpass off MLK wrote: LIFE BEGINS AT 100, hit the Rockridge BART underpass wrote: ALIENS

HAVE GENTRIFIED EARTH, scrolled over to some trains parked on the tracks in Albany, wrote: THE UNIVERSE IS A MODEL OF ITSELF, swam over to the lower bottoms hit a warehouse, wrote: PEACE ALLAH, cut over to an abandoned storefront deep east international, wrote: FICTION IS REAL, whipped up to Indian Rock, wrote, STOLEN LAND, hit the abandoned movie theater in Emeryville wrote, PUNK'S NOT DEAD, hit the West Grand 880 entrance wrote TRUTH N BOOTY, and so and so forth, it was a nite of mad ups, the dawn came cracking on forward and we cadets of this grand spaceship earth broke on thru to another side as per usual.

80.

I was posted up on the couch in a sunny patch catching the late afternoon rays, drifting in and out of sleep, Khadija in deep meditation, Fatima and Madonna hard at work on their blueprints, Fausto off playing dice somewhere.

My phone rang.

"Hello?"

"Hola, Mohammad X?"

"Si, ¿quien es?"

"Soy yo, Enrique Peña-Nieto, El Presidente de Mexico."

"Conyo cabrón."

"¿Prefieres que hablemos en Ingles?"

"Yeah."

"I call to ask you a favor."

"Word?"

"I heard you were the best."

"I am."

"I need to send you on a Mission of Diplomacy."

"No doubt."

"I've chartered you a private flight to the sun to discuss some matters of security with Huitzilopochtli."

"Oh word?"

"I can't say much more. There should be a chauffeur knocking on your door right now."

Knock knock.

Damn, the Mexican government was on point when they wanted to be. And literally only then.

I kissed my daughters on they lil foreheads and kizzed my wife on her lips and climbed in the hired vehicle over to a military airport and boarded a private flight to the sun.

The sun was hot as fuck. Bruh, it was hella hot. Damn.

I was led into Huitzilopochtli's Oval Office. AC was on full blast but it was still like irritatingly warm I scooted to the edge of the hot ass leather couch over to where I was directly under an air vent catch that cool AC breeze. Phew. Now where were we?

Huitzilopochtli spake first:

"I declare eternal war."

"On who?"

"All existence."

Wasn't that already the deal? I asked: "Why?"

"The children of the Sun have begged their father for their own destruction!"

Story seemed to check out.

"I've been hired to convince u to chill."

"The sun don't chill Allah."

"Then it seems we're at an impasse."

"Yes, I've arranged for ur swift return home, my regards to Señor Presidente and his wife."

I was dropped off back at the crib.

The minute I opened the door, the phone rang.

"Hola!"

"You have failed me."

"Lo siento, Señor Presidente, his mind was made up."

"I was told you were the best."

"I am."

"No you're not."

"I guess we can chalk it up to a difference of opinion."

"We're doomed."

"What's new?"

"Ay! Ay! Ay!"

"Canta, no llores, Señor Presidente."

The presidente cleared his throat and began to croon:

Vitzilopuchi, yaquetlaya, yyaconay, ynohuihuihuia: anenicuic, toçiquemitla, yya, ayya, yya y ya uia, queyanoca, oya tonaqui, yyaya, yya, yya.

Tetzauiztli ya mixtecatl, ce ymocxi pichauaztecatla pomaya, ouayyeo, ayyayya.

Ay tlaxotla tenamitl yuitli macoc mupupuxotiuh, yautlatoa ya, ayyayyo, noteuh aya tepanquizqui mitoaya.

Oya yeua uel mamauia, in tlaxotecatl teuhtla milacatzoaya, itlaxotecatl teuhtla milacatzoaya.

Amanteca toyauan xinechoncentlalizquiuia ycalipan yauhtiua, xinechoncentlalizqui.

Pipiteca toyauan xinechoncentlalizquiuia: ycalipan. yautiua, xinechoncentlalizqui.

His voice was remarkably beautiful, I was surprised.

"You know what, that did make me feel better."

"Glad to hear it mane."

"I will send you a gift."

Knock, knock.

Opened the door to a Mexican secret service agent in a black suit and Ray Bans unclicking himself from a briefcase he had been handcuffed to. He handed me the briefcase, saluted me and bounced. I opened the briefcase: 1 Million Pesos (55k USD).

Not bad for a day's work.

81.

We were at Juan and Amadea's baby shower. I gave them a million pesos. I drank like five beers with three expats, one Chicano dude Eric, a vet, one Scottish dude MacNuff (fake name, ex con), and one retired computer white dude I forget his name.

There was hella kids there, Fatima, Madonna, Lupe and Rosa were socializing with all them. They were surprisingly good at it.

Groovy time.

Afterwards we went and copped a Golden State Warriors Calavera and a blown glass bong.

Went back to the crib, got stoned off the new bong, watched Fantastic Mr. Fox with Fatima and Madonna.

Made quesadillas.

Maestro slid thru w Maria, Lupe and Rosa.

We drank beers and smoked weed, listened to Ells Regina out on the deck, looked up at the stars while the kids watched Fantastic Mr. Fox again.

Maestro Hakim Karim Karim Hakim Allah played I Shall Be Released on the guitar we each wept a single tear, except Maria who wept two hundred tears, one hundred out of her left eye for Rosa and one hundred out of her right eye for Lupe. As she cried she spake:

SOSIRIBAOE ILLALE YABUMBAO LLALE IMILATE ALLAVA OMIO EKO ILLALE YAMUBAO LLALE OMILATE ALLAVA OMIO AGUAREKE AGUAKELONA HE YEMAYA AGUAREKE AGUAKUELONA HE YEMAYA AGUAGUELONA HE AGUAREKE ASTARAFIO OLOCUM DALE COLLUMLA HA MI PA OMIO EKO LLALE YA LLUMBAO LLALE OMILATE ALLAVA OMIO YEMAYA AO OLOCUM ABOKO MI YEMAYA YEMAYA HO OLOCUN ABOKO YEMAYA TIRAZECUM TIRALECUM TIRALECUM ABO YEMAYA YEMAYA LORDE ABOKO HAR HE LLALORDE LLALORDE HE YEMAYA LORDE ABOKO HAE ABOKO LARIOTE LARI OTE OTE OTE YEMAYA LORDE LARI OTE LARI OTE LARIO LARIO LARI OTE LARI OTE OTE OTE LARIO LARIO OTE

We all wept 300 more tears a piece. Maestro Hakim and Maria departed with Lupe and Rosa. Khadija put Fatima to bed and I recited a rosary like: Ave Maria full o' grace the lordt is wit thee, #blessed art thou among wymin & blezzed B Tha fr00t uv thy womb jeezy Santa Maria Madre de Dios prayer hands emoji 4 R zinnerz now + @ th'hour o' our defs en el nombre Del padre el hijo el espirtu santo etc.

It began to rain furiously, a tempest, electrical, thunder, CHANGO.

I said:

CHANGO MANI COTE CHANGO MANI COTE OLLE MASA CHANGO MANI COTE OLLE MASA CHANGO ARA BARI COTE CHANGO ARABARICOTE ODE MATA ICOTE ALAMA SOICOTE YE ADA MANICOTE ADA MANICOTE ARAN BANSONI CHANGO MANI COTE CHANGO MANI COTE ELLE MASA CHANGO ARAMBSONI CHANGO ARA BARICOTE ODEMATA ICOTE SONI SORI CHANGO ARABARICOTE ARABARICOTE ARA SORI HE HE LELE AGUO GUE GUE ARO A MAYO GUERA HE HE GUE GUE HA MAYO AMAYO GUERA OKOKOTE ARO EGUE ARO AMAYO GUERA MANICOTE CHANGO MANICOTE OYE MATE MANICOTE OYE MATA ALABAO CHANGO ARABARICOTE CHANGO ARABARICOTE ALAGUAO BARICOTE OYE MATA ARABARIOCOTE SORI ACHE CHANGO MANI COTE SOICOTE ARA ADOMEMATA ODE ODE ODEMATA ODE ODE OYE MATA ARA BARICOTE SORI SORI SORI ODE MATA ODE MATA SORI ACHE BARICOTE ARA BARICOTE SORI ACHE CHANGO

I was soaked in rain, the waves were two stories high, crashing furiously.

Bruh.

82.

Woke up checked my bank account. Zero dollars. I called up my bank and let them have it:

"Word life reality peace god immaculate build/destroy wisdom infinite. Ain't no justice, just us, this be the Godbody, Allah is just. The laws of man crumble in the faces of Gods, the laws of Gods crumble in they own faces, the faces crumble into laws, a law is a law, Allah is Allah, God is God, Love is Love, It Is what It Is, Everything is Everything. All praises due to the most high Jah Rastafari, Allah Hu Akbar Chango Yemaya. I am the word made flesh, I'm a person, I'm a sound, now I have become destroyer of worlds, I have become light and paper, vapor within ur mind. I am u, ur me, we are all together, ur positivity is my positivity, ur negativity is my negativity, my refusal to recognize a positive truth within myself and vice versa. I don't care about the edges or the details I want the root glowing in the middle, the heaving oceans of tranquility located at the center, I want us all to get there, the specificities of this earthly realm grow tiresome, wash me in the waters of the super soul and free me from the confines of this flesh, strip away the interference,or whatever, do whatever, the earthly realm has its little charms. Bruh!"

"Yes sir!"

I hung up, checked my balance again: 1 million pesos (~55k USD).

No doubt, no doubt.

It was still raining, been raining for like two days straight. El Niño relieving the Pacific Coastal drought to some degree.

I stayed inside and flipped thru some Charles Bukowski poems, then the Bhagavad Gita, then a Spanish Translation of The Alchemist, then a Bukowski novel, then Voodoo in Haiti, then The Masaryk Case.

The written word grew tiresome to ur boy and I smoked some tree watched an episode of the Bernie Mac show.

Khadija put on Francoise Hardy again and started dancing around.

I smoked more weed out that new bong.

I was wearing sweatpants. Felt like Earl Sweatpants.

Flipped channels:

Fieri, Bourdain, Ansari, Kardashian, Hilton, Trump, ISIS, Sanders, Clinton, Obama, Warriors beating the 'sixers.

We turned off the TV and mediated for 7 hours, then drank some Uña de Gato tea.

I went back to reading the Masaryk Case, it read like an old Lorca play; measured, rich, dense.

I felt a strange rush of intense sorrow, felt it intensely for a moment and let it pass.

Hit the bong again.

Watched Sailor Moon with Fatima and Madonna while Khadija took a nap.

The rain wouldn't let up.

I fell asleep.

Woke up to Khadija, Fatima and Madonna dancing to Janet Jackson. Fell back asleep. Woke up to Khadija bringing me coffee and a joint. Fatima and Madonna were asleep. Fausto off Allah knows where, gamblin', his chip stack raising ever higher.

We got stoned, listened to the same side of whatever lil jazz record we had last left on, kissed around, did our thing, fell asleep, another rainy day on earth, mane, they don't stop, they just keep comin'.

83.

Hopped up out of bed, turned my swag on. Took a look in the mirror, said: "what up, yeah, we gettin money."

Strapped two iguanas to my feet, roller-skated over to Alameda, parked on a bench under an orange tree in a secluded corner of a suburban park, meditated.

People peopled on by, bees circumnavigated they lil flower bushes. Squirrels, thrushes, game birds, rustled in the trees. Puppies panted by. I watched the lil milieu unfold.

A green parrot landed in front of me and sang:

"The time of man nears an end!"

I responded: "Ay!"

"The time of time is almost nigh!"

"Woo!"

"The time of space approaches implosion!"

"Swag! Swag!"

"The jewel of being glitters then sizzles away into infinity!"

"Bless up!"

"Break on thru to the other side!"

"Praise Jah!"

"Don't you want somebody to love?"

"Allah Hu Akbar!"

"Don't you need somebody to love?"

"Allah Hu Akbar!"

"Would you love somebody to love?"

"Allah Hu Akbar!"

"U betta find somebody to love!"

"Jah Rastafari!"

"All the way turnt up!"

"Turn up, turn up!"

"Swag infinity!"
"Swag! Swag! Swag!"
"Truth on truth!"
"The joy of our supersoul pervades!"
>>>
...
The day carried on in that fashion.

No new truths were created nor were old truths destroyed just that selfsame truth of always in perpetual flux.

84.

I rose from my gilt sarcophagus, took a speed pill and a shot of tequila, hit the bong, did the dishes, thinking "The prophet is blue," whatever that means. Did 100 push-ups and 200 sit-ups. Made some eggs and tomatoes and Lapsang Souchong tea.

Mijo Fausto out there in some casino, counting his winnings.

Fatima, Madonna and Khadija woke up finally and we had breakfast out on the deck, it had finally stopped raining, everything was still damp and drying off but it was sunny and warm, felt tropical.

We went down to the beach, I jumped in, wild cold, got out and dried out on a towel. The sand was mildly damp.

The waves were there doing the same thing they had been doing for a couple hundred million years or so, same look, same sound, most of that time without anybody looking at them. People looking at the ocean is still a relatively new thing on earth.

We walked along the cliffs til the lite changed, then we cut back. By the time we got home the wind was wild. Wild was the wind.

We listened to Wild is the Wind by Nina Simone then tried to learn it on acoustic guitar. Got it down OK but it needed some work. Listened to the Bowie version. Solid work.

I put on seminal 1968 Ornette Coleman album Free Jazz, my all time favorite record maybe.

Afterwards I climbed the hill alone and looked at the stars in silence. Silence is still the most beautiful and sacred music. It's so beautiful it's hard to take sometimes. So, like, hence, music.

I came back down the hill did 100 more push-ups and 200 more sit-ups. Strapped on two iguanas and rollerbladed over to the Oxxo, stole a Coca-Cola, skated down the strip, traded my iguanas for one bigger iguana, tested it out with a kick flip, tight, everything seemed to be in order. Skated down the strip, copped a super swaggy Yurple velvet mariachi sombrero with the gold embroidery, 50/50 grinded a 14 stair rail, copped some painkillers.

Skated back up to the house, put the Coca-Cola on the Huitzilopochtli altar, fell asleep.

Woke up early, hit of tequila, speed pill, painkiller, bong rips, do the dishes, push-ups, sit-ups, shower, beach, shower, more drugs, beer, next day no drugs, no alcohol, read Proust, next day smoked weed and drank ice tea all day listening to 'Trane, next day we went horseback riding, next day we took a boat ride, next day it was raining and we kicked inside drinking coffee and chiefin tree watching TV, next day meditation all day with breaks for tea, next day was hot as fuck we just kicked it at the beach, hella other days occurred.

The whole time, Fatima and Madonna found time to work on they blueprints for The Beautiful Everything. They were toying with the name, was weighing The Beautiful Perfect Everything against The Perfect Beautiful Everything. As impressive as the thing itself, they had invented a number of components to The Beautiful Perfect Everything, highly ingenious stuff, had jiggered out the figures of what looked to be a flawless Flux Apprehension System, a Chaos Loop Harness the likes of which prior unseen to man, and a Multi-Perpetuation Engine that was truly unprecedented. Their concepts were more than sound, they were lightspeed, infinite, perfectly brilliant.

And one day they were done, and the work reflected all eternity back, the work was the beginning and ending of an infinite multiplicatorial verse, the ever pulsating cosmic supersoul, they had invented existence itself, existence inventing itself.

Their invention was worth a great deal of money, they had investors lining up, trying to figure out how to rope and ride the pony, how to market the eternal concept, we hired a legal team, a marketing consultant, an accountant, and a general business manager. The money rolled right in. Fatima and Madonna (and their shareholding partners Lupe & Rosa) had struck gold, they had broken the 7th wall, the self, the container of existence, they had invented the very concept of transcendence basically, without even lifting so much as a finger, we were rich, we re-did the bathrooms and the kitchen, imported Madagascan Baobob wood floors, painted the house a new brute white, we spent our days simply guiding our psychic energy this way or that, absorbing sea, sun moon stars, air, rain, gardening, walking swimming, breathing, meditating. We had won, we had built Freedom. The sun had risen again from here and again from here it would rise again from here again.

85.

I was driving an '85 Jeep Scrambler thru Santa Sirena when I realized I was in Paradise Hills. Santa Sirena is Paradise Hills and Paradise Hills is Santa Sirena. We had never left Paradise, it's impossible to leave Paradise because Paradise is eternally wherever it is ur headed. What a trip man.

I pulled up to the crib, Khadija had already grown tired of her last paint job and had painted the entire place a vivid hot pink. It looked beautiful, radically different. There's was an entire third floor I had never noticed. It's amazing what a new coat of paint will do.

I rolled into the crib all like, "Honey, I'm home!"

Wifey gave me a peck on my mouth and cut me off from explaining to her what she apparently already knew:

"I know what ur going to say, we're living in paradise."

Huh. Go figure.

I sat down watched some old rerun of "I Love Lucy" set to work carving a self portrait in Ebony.

It started to lightly snow outside, I bundled up walked over to the stable and saddled up my trusty brown steed Copernicus for a ride thru the wood.

Found a lil trail lined with snow-dusted evergreens.

Whose woods these were I thought I knew.

They were mine.

I watched them fill up with snow.

My little horse must have thought it queer

To stop without a farmhouse near

Between the woods and frozen lake

The darkest evening of the year.

He gave his lil harness bells a shake

To ask if there wuz some mistake.

The only other sound, the sweep

Of easy wind and downy flake.

The woods were lovely, dark and deep,

But I had promises to keep,

And miles to go before I could sleep,

Bruh,

And miles to go before I could sleep.

Bruh.

So I trotted on, mane.

Midway upon the journey,

I found myself within a forest dark,

For the straightforward pathway had been lost.

Ah me! how hard a thing it is to say

What was this forest savage, rough, and stern,

Which in the very thought renews the fear.

So bitter is it, death is little more;

But of the good to treat, which there I found,

Speak will I of the other things I saw there.

I cannot well repeat how there I entered,

So full was I of slumber at the moment
In which I had abandoned the true way.
But after I had reached a mountain's foot,
At that point where the valley terminated,
Which had with consternation pierced my heart,
Upward I looked, and I beheld its shoulders,
Vested already with that planet's rays
Which leadeth others right by every road.
Then was the fear a little quieted
That in my heart's lake had endured throughout
The night, which I had passed so piteously.
And even as he, who, with distressful breath,
Forth issued from the sea upon the shore,
Turns to the water perilous and gazes;
So did my soul, that still was fleeing onward,
Turn itself back to re-behold the pass
Which never yet a living person left.
After my weary body I had rested,
The way resumed I on the desert slope,
So that the firm foot ever was the lower.
And lo! almost where the ascent began,
A panther light and swift exceedingly,
Which with a spotted skin was covered o'er!
And never moved she from before my face,
Nay, rather did impede so much my way,
That many times I to return had turned.
The time was the beginning of the morning,
And up the sun was mounting with those stars
That with him were, what time the Love Divine
At first in motion set those beauteous things;
So were to me occasion of good hope,
The variegated skin of that wild beast,

The hour of time, and the delicious season;
But not so much, that did not give me fear
A lion's aspect which appeared to me.
He seemed as if against me he were coming
With head uplifted, and with ravenous hunger,
So that it seemed the air was afraid of him;
And a she-wolf, that with all hungerings
Seemed to be laden in her meagreness,
And many folk has caused to live forlorn!
She brought upon me so much heaviness,
With the affright that from her aspect came,
That I the hope relinquished of the height.
And as he is who willingly acquires,
And the time comes that causes him to lose,
Who weeps in all his thoughts and is despondent,
E'en such made me that beast withouten peace,
Which, coming on against me by degrees
Thrust me back thither where the sun is silent.
While I was rushing downward to the lowland,
Before mine eyes did one present himself,
Who seemed from long-continued silence hoarse.
When I beheld him in the desert vast,
"Have pity on me," unto him I cried,
"Whiche'er thou art, or shade or real man!"
He answered me: "Not man; man once I was,
And both my parents were of Lombardy,
And Mantuans by country both of them.
'Sub Julio' was I born, though it was late,
And lived at Rome under the good Augustus,
During the time of false and lying gods.
A poet was I, and I sang that just
Son of Anchises, who came forth from Troy,

After that Ilion the superb was burned.
But thou, why goest thou back to such annoyance?
Why climb'st thou not the Mount Delectable,
Which is the source and cause of every joy?"
"Now, art thou that Virgilius and that fountain
Which spreads abroad so wide a river of speech?"
I made response to him with bashful forehead.
"O, of the other poets honour and light,
Avail me the long study and great love
That have impelled me to explore thy volume!
Thou art my master, and my author thou,
Thou art alone the one from whom I took
The beautiful style that has done honour to me.
Behold the beast, for which I have turned back;
Do thou protect me from her, famous Sage,
For she doth make my veins and pulses tremble."
"Thee it behoves to take another road,"
Responded he, when he beheld me weeping,
"If from this savage place thou wouldst escape;
Because this beast, at which thou criest out,
Suffers not any one to pass her way,
But so doth harass him, that she destroys him;
And has a nature so malign and ruthless,
That never doth she glut her greedy will,
And after food is hungrier than before.
Many the animals with whom she weds,
And more they shall be still, until the Greyhound
Comes, who shall make her perish in her pain.
He shall not feed on either earth or pelf,
But upon wisdom, and on love and virtue;
'Twixt Feltro and Feltro shall his nation be;
Of that low Italy shall he be the saviour,

On whose account the maid Camilla died,
Euryalus, Turnus, Nisus, of their wounds;
Through every city shall he hunt her down,
Until he shall have driven her back to Hell,
There from whence envy first did let her loose.
Therefore I think and judge it for thy best
Thou follow me, and I will be thy guide,
And lead thee hence through the eternal place,
Where thou shalt hear the desperate lamentations,
Shalt see the ancient spirits disconsolate,
Who cry out each one for the second death;
And thou shalt see those who contented are
Within the fire, because they hope to come,
Whene'er it may be, to the blessed people;
To whom, then, if thou wishest to ascend,
A soul shall be for that than I more worthy;
With her at my departure I will leave thee;
Because that Emperor, who reigns above,
In that I was rebellious to his law,
Wills that through me none come into his city.
He governs everywhere, and there he reigns;
There is his city and his lofty throne;
O happy he whom thereto he elects!"
And I to him: "Poet, I thee entreat,
By that same God whom thou didst never know,
So that I may escape this woe and worse,
Thou wouldst conduct me there where thou hast said,
That I may see the portal of Saint Peter,
And those thou makest so disconsolate."
Then he moved on, and I behind him followed.
Ended up back at the crib somehow.
Wifey was like "Ay, our palm wine tapster has died."

"Fuck!"

"We have to follow him into The Land of the Dead."

"U right, u right."

So we climbed on our flying carpet with Tima and journeyed to The Land of the Dead over in Chapter 86.

86.

We were in The Land of the Dead, searching for our palm wine tapster.

A tall jungle spirit came up to us asking for money, I gave him every coin in my pocket, 63 pesos, he ran off wooping.

A flying jungle spirit apparitioned, hovering before us. I gave her all the cash I had, 420 pesos, she flew off wooping.

A short jungle spirit ran up like "gimme all ur money."

I was like "peace Allah"

He punched me in the face then I beat the shit out of him. We started to walk away but he just popped up, dusted himself off and ran at me again, landing another punch that made me dizzy. I beat the shit out of him again but he landed hella more punches this time, definitely starting to hurt, tire me out, wear me down. My wife and daughters gazed on and screamed, they could do nothing, it was against the law for women to fight in The Land of the Dead.

When I thought it was over and started to walk away he sprang up again and ran up on me again, swinging and landing good ones, almost got my ass kicked but managed to kick his ass again. He got up again. We fought some more. This time I beat him to death.

I started to walk away and he rose from the dead started punching the shit out of me. I had to keep punching him back the whole time thinking "holy shit, I can't kill this fool he's already dead." I was starting to ache and grow tired, his punches were landing and growing with strength and accuracy. The old rope a dope.

The nightmarish truth of this concept was just starting to sink in when that first jungle spirit I had kicked 63 pesos to happened by. This was the land of the dead, so of course he was dead too so when he swooped in and beat the short jungle spirit to death, the short jungle spirit died for real this time. Because the only way the dead can die in The Land of the Dead is when another dead kills them. He was gone now, the short jungle spirit, he was nothing. See when u die, u go to the land of the dead, but when u die in the land of the dead, u don't go anywhere. Ur just dead, nothing. Disappeared. The tall spirit gave me my 63 pesos back: "Ur gona need this out here."

Dude, the land of the dead is hella crazy.

We continued on…

Came across a sick flea market copped some peanuts, munched on those and browsed the selection of knick knacks, bought a pipe carved out of a blue painted skull and copped some red fern, came to 33 pesos. Walked over to a waterfall, got high, we all went swimming in the yurple waves neath the prismatic waterfall.

Walked some more and came across a tiny jungle spirit running some kind of 3 card monty hustle, I put 3 pesos down:

"There's 3 cards, see? The six which is equality, the eight which is build or destroy and the blank card, which is nada, nothing, zero, cypher complete. U pick the 6, ur 3 become 18, u pick the 8, ur 3 become 24, u pick the blank and I keep that 3 right there."

He shuffled, and I watched, lost track, took a wild guess, it was an 8, I was up 21. Played again, hit a 6, was up 141, decided to quit while I was ahead.

"Oh no u don't."

The Monty spirit pulled a shank on ur boy.

Tall jungle spirit rolled up like "bop" duffed yung Monty spirit out.

I kicked him 126 pesos. I was still up 15. Not bad.

Ran along thru the jungle, came to a banana grove. Built a lil lean-too out of banana wood and thatched banana leaves. 'Tima and 'Donna designed it. Me and 'Dija were just her laborers.

It ended up looking tight, we had a simple dinner of bananas and fell asleep in our banana leaf hammocks., it started to rain but the roof didn't leak. 'Tima and 'Donna were truly master architects.

The next morning we carried on, ended up at a 7/11 went in to cop a lil sixer of Pacifico, dude behind the counter was the tapster, I was like "Bruh."

He was like "Bruh."

I copped some King Sized Zig Zags and cut.

We made it home alive, peace Allah JAH Rasta, CHANGO.

87.

I was on the deck drinking tequila taking bong rips with Maestro Karim Hakim Hakim Karim Allah.

'Tima, 'Donna and 'Dija were on a walk. Maria, Lupe, Rosa off in town or something.

Maestro was shitting on the shades of magical realism in Doestoyevski's Karamazov Bros:

"I don't fuck with no book where the man die and just fly off to heaven right out the window."

"That happen in Karamazov Bros? I never finished it."

"It happened closer to the beginning."

"I quit that book early. Very good just a little too boring."

"Well I don't care for it."

We had our abacuses out and did some number crunching, he had some new post-algebraic theorems he wanted me to plug thru and see if they held some water. I ran the numbers and it all seemed to hold up.

Would have to test them in the dream realm too, who knows how long that would take.

It was all recreational, my genius daughters had already thought the Great Thoughts we were just having some fun filling in the blanks.

Fausto gambled his way across the casinos of earth, delighting in all of the mortal pleasures.

Tima, Donna and Dija came back. Maestro made carrot juice for everybody I mixed mine with tequila. It was wonderful, mane. I called it a Mexican Thai Iced Tea.

Mane, it's them lil thangz

What's life but a string of moments, some sick, some trill, some tru, some swaggy, some tight, some loose, some lit, some faded, some dope, some fresh, some sweet, some chill, some ill, some rad, some bogus, some gnarly, some turnt up, some most excellent, some sublime, some divine, some spectacular, some uncanny, some eerie, some ironic, some grotesque, some supernatural , some surreal, some iconic, some hyper real, some wavy, some maney, some groovy, some joogy, some jiggy, some swiggy, some real cool, some cut pool, some jazz joon, some twirling, some swirling, some smiling, some spiraling, all ever same, beaming, zooming, glorious, yeah baby, groovy, damn son, where'd u find this, Allah, JAH Rasta, CHANGO.

Man we were humming trigonomically, the earth was zipping along at a thousand miles an hour and peso-to-dollar ratio was close to 20. Gold was up, whisky was gearing for what looked to be a big spike, the Warriors beat the Thunder, the Panthers beat the Broncos.

Life is a numbers game, sadly, and then also, happily enough too I guess. The abacus beads clacked in the mellow afternoon sun, pencil scritching realities along sheaths of papyrus.

The afternoon sun, the afternoon sun.

Oh what a funky feeling.

Maestro Allah packed up and cut.

I went down to the beach with the wife and kid. We dunked and swam in the waters, El Pacifico.

We soaked that sun and sea up for a couple hours came back.

Me and Dija went on the Internet. Dija had chopped down the roof satellite a while back so we now surfed the net from the meditational browsers of our own subjective consciousnesses, it was a pure internet connection, soul plugged into super soul.

Tima and Donna wandered off to work on their blueprints, they found the Internet to be boring, they had to tinker with some aspects of the Perfect Beautiful Everything.

For the first time in a while, I felt like, restless, like I should be doing something.

Then I felt too tired to do anything and fell into a deep yogic sleep. When I woke up Dija, Donna and Tima were mediating together.

I did some stretches and push-ups and sit-ups and meditated.

That Internet had really worn a player out. Then I remembered there is no difference between anything and pow! I was back up and at 'em, pep in my step, etc.

I drove out to Triviadero and played some cards w my nigga Falstaff the welder, his two homies from trade school and his bro in the Mexican Army. I won like 900 pesos, wuzat like 70 bux? The dollar was decent at the moment.

Slid back home scooped some fresh wood-smoked tamales on the way back, the smoke from the fire hit my eyes and I cried a touch, felt cool.

Came back, we all supped on tamales.

Dija, Donna and Tima set to meditating again and I cut out to the bar. All the old timers were there watching a big futbol match on TV, the Santa Sirena Delfines versus their long time rivals the Santa Alazne Diablitos.

Delfines were losing, as usual. Score was 0-2. The mood was subdued with a slight crackle of tension, but mostly just the patent resigned solemnity of the underdog sports bar fly.

A chihuahua was scrambling around, drunk, lightening the mood, entertaining everybody. He was the belle of the ball, his cute buggy eyes, his jittery demeanor, his unsure lil paws clacking against the old brown tile floor. The dog was clowning, standing, dancing, slipping, falling, taking sips of everybody's beers, singing along to the commercial jingles, hamming it up, enjoying the spotlight. U had to hand it to the dog, perfect canine cheerleader, drunk diminutive lil mascot he wuz, he brought cheer when cheer was needed, k Dios le bendiga mane.

88.

It was morning, we were getting breakfast at a local gringo expat eatery. Huevos, frijoles, tortillas papas, cafe y whatnot.

The sun was shining hit thru the palm treez. I took off my sunglasses. Whew. I put my sunglasses back on. Phew.

Old gringo expat longhair hippie was playing Led Zeppelin on acoustic guitar, he was sick widdit.

I think I had been drinking the day before, I think, I don't even remember.

Oh yea it was that futbol game. We lost 3 to 1. That one goal got us hype tho. We was off that tequila. Everybody knew my name at that bar, and I knew all their faces.

Thought vaguely about the mathematical nature of existence, sipped some cafe.

I'm bad at math that's probably why it comes off as so magical to the kid.

Gringo expats have skrong psychic energy, I was soaking that up.

I had been off the swine mostly since my conversion to Islam in Chapter 1 but I ordered some tocino. When in Rome.

Bruh so here we are: Chapter 88.

Peace to Amaze 88.

If ur reading this novel O.K. alongside its musical soundtrack, the 100 song KOOL A.D. album of the same name, the corresponding song to this chapter is called: FREAKIN OUT, a Talking Heads-ish number wherein the vocalist, one Victor "KOOL A.D." Vazquez (me) repeatedly asks the listener if he or she is "freaking out." It's more or less a rhetorical question.

Kick back and listen that tune right now.

That's a good one, right?

We headed home, Tima and Donna took a nap, Dija meditated and I hit the bong and did 50 push-ups, hit the bong again, took a shower, took a nap.

Woke up sober finally. Breaking the 4th wall took it out of ur boy, I was pooped. Watched an episode of M.A.S.H., that perked me up, played on the old Mexican acoustic El Maestro had lent me. Hotel California by the Eagles. Not familiar with most of their work but that one song is fire.

Pulled back the needle and started the record that was left on the the turntable: Billie Holiday's Greatest Hits.

Felt old timey.

Kicked it in that radiant late morning sunshine waiting for Chapter 89.

89.

Me and wife woke up, walked down the hill to the ocean, jumped in naked, swam into a school of 89 dolphins, they were all naked too.

The babies had created their own babysitter, The Perfect Beautiful Everything. Plus also, Malika was kicking it with them, she was in town on some business.

Anyway, me and wife swam around the seas of Baja within this school of 89 dolphins, we felt the joy ecstatic mane I tell u.

We were peace. We were and are.

I was like:

a kick in the air
a kick in the air
let me cook
how shall i put it
here's how it was put to me:
"hercules, hercules"
the party line
love, vampiric, romantic, harmonies
the burdens of peace and comfort
how free is free
sadness, donuts
entropy is ubiquitous
poetry is the concept of all bars
marijuana is a wise plant
potatoes are a tasty root
water, ice cubes
the freeways, the pyramids
the geodesic domes of ur imaginariums

this is a sweet poem, no?

She was like: U right u right tru tru no doubt no doubt word ok

I was like: peace Allah JAH Rasta fari CHANGO

She was like:

Allah Allah

Hare Krishna

YEMAYA

Ave Maria

We swam for 7 days, on the 8th day my arms grew weak and we stopped at an island.

We cracked some coconuts with our bare Kung fu hands and drank their sweet water.

The sun was wild radiant fam.

The sky was hella blue.

The palm trees swayed in the breeze.

Big leaves of grass, big rubber leaves, hella green leaves of all varietals, a parrot here, a leaping dauphinois off in the dist.

Paradise, mane.

Every second contains paradise.

She hummed I sung, the sun beat down on us then gave up and the moon gave us a nice lil hug and a kiss.

The waters lapped, ceaseless.

90.

I was like:

Comrade,

I've just finished reading [redacted]'s analysis of fascism (she's a brilliant, "big," beautiful revolutionary woman—ain't she!!) I've studied ur letters on the subject carefully. it could be productive for the 3 of us to get together at once and subject the whole question to a detailed historical analysis. There is some difference of opinion and interpretation of history between us, but basically I think we are brought together on the principal points by the fact that the three of us could not meet without probably causing world war 3.

give her my deepest and warmest love and ask her to review these comments. this is not all that i will have to say on the subject. i'll constantly return to myself and reexamine. i expect i will have to carry this on for another couple of hundred pages. We'll deal with the questions as they come up, but for now this should provoke both of u to push me on to a greater effort.

the basis of [BUFFERING]'s analysis is tied into several old left notions that are at least open to some question now. it is my view that out of the economic crisis of the last great depression, fascism-corporativism, did indeed emerge, develop and consolidate itself into its most advanced form here in Amerika. In the process, socialist consciousness suffered from very severe setbacks. Unlike [BUFFERING], I do not believe that this realization leads to a defeatist view of history.

An understanding of the reality of our situation is essential to the success of future revolutionizing activity. To contend that corporativism has emerged and advanced is not to say that it has triumphed. We are not defeated. Pure fascism, absolute totalitarianism, is not possible.

Heirarchy has had six thousand years of trial. It will never succeed for long in any form. Fascism and its historical significance is the point of my whole philosophy on politics and its extension, war. My opinion is that we are at the historical climax (the flash point) of the totalitarian period. The analysis in depth that the subject deserves has yet to be done.

She was like:

What happened at the New Wil'ins? Bitch, I'm back by popular demand Y'all haters corny with that Illuminati mess Paparazzi, catch my fly, and my cocky fresh I'm so reckless when I rock my Givenchy dress (stylin') I'm so possessive so I rock his Roc necklaces My daddy Alabama, Momma Louisiana You mix that negro with that Creole make a Texas bama I like my baby heir with baby hair and afros I like my negro nose with Jackson Five nostrils Earned all this money but they never take the country out me I got a hot sauce in my bag, swag Oh yeah, baby, oh yeah I, ohhhhh, oh, yes, I like that I did not come to play with you hoes, haha I came to slay, bitch I like cornbreads and collard greens, bitch Oh, yes, you besta believe it Y'all haters corny with that illuminati mess Paparazzi, catch my fly, and my cocky fresh I'm so reckless when I rock my Givenchy dress (stylin') I'm so possessive so I rock his Roc necklaces My daddy Alabama, Momma Louisiana You mix that negro with that Creole make a Texas bama I like my baby heir with baby hair and afros I like my negro nose with Jackson Five nostrils Earned all this money but they never take the country out me I got a hot sauce in my bag, swag I see it, I want it, I stunt, yellow-bone it I dream it, I work hard, I grind 'til I own it I twirl on them haters, albino alligators El Camino with the seat low, sippin' Cuervo with no chaser Sometimes I go off (I go off), I go hard (I go hard) Get what's mine (take what's mine), I'm a star (I'm a star) Cause I slay (slay), I slay (hey), I slay (okay), I slay (okay) All day (okay), I slay (okay), I slay (okay), I slay (okay) We gon' slay (slay), gon' slay (okay), we slay (okay), I slay (okay) I slay (okay), okay (okay), I slay (okay), okay, okay, okay, okay Okay, okay, ladies, now let's get in formation, cause I slay Okay, ladies, now let's get in formation, cause I slay Prove to me you got some coordination, cause I slay Slay trick, or you get eliminated When he fuck me good I take his ass to Red Lobster, cause I slay When he fuck me good I take his ass to Red Lobster, cause I slay If he hit it right, I might take him on a flight on my chopper, cause I slay Drop him off at the mall, let him buy some J's, let him shop up, cause I slay I might get your song played on the radio station, cause I slay I might get your song played on the radio station, cause I slay You just might be a black Bill Gates in the making, cause I slay I just might be a black Bill Gates in the making I see it, I want it, I stunt, yellow-bone it I dream it, I work hard, I grind 'til I own it I twirl on my haters, albino alligators El Camino with the seat low, sippin' Cuervo with no chaser Sometimes I go off (I go off), I go hard (I go hard) Get what's mine (take what's mine), I'm a star (I'm a star) Cause I slay (slay), I slay (hey), I slay (okay), I slay (okay) All day (okay), I slay (okay), I slay (okay), I slay (okay) We gon' slay (slay), gon' slay (okay), we slay (okay), I slay (okay) I slay (okay), okay (okay), I slay (okay), okay, okay, okay, okay Okay, okay, ladies, now let's get in formation, cause I slay Okay, ladies, now let's get in formation, cause I slay Prove to me you got some coordination, cause I slay Slay trick, or you get eliminated Okay, ladies, now let's get in formation, I slay Okay, ladies, now let's get in formation You know you that bitch when you cause all this conversation Always stay gracious, best revenge is your paper Girl, I hear some thunder Golly, look at that water, boy, oh lord

Phone rang, saved by the bell, "hold up I gota take a call, hello?"

"MOHAMMAD X, it's Ricky from Al Jazeera, is now a good time to talk?"

"Talk about what? No, now's not a good time."

"About Israel and Palestine, we had arranged on this exact time for this interview."

"We did? Oh snap well ok fire away then."

"Don't u think ur doing a half ass job at keeping the Israelis from killing the Palestinians?"

"Well, that's a good question, and funny u should ask that question cause a matter of fact yes I do feel like I'm doing a shitty job keeping the Israelis from killing the Palestinians, the numbers are totally fucked and only getting worse, men women and children are being needlessly slaughtered by an globally illegal and illegitimate occupying imperialist, colonialist regime but see there's only so much unpaid effort, energy and other subjective forms of personal capital I can put into the matter as a single individual."

"I thought u didn't believe in capital."

"I don't believe in capital per se or a priori but I do occasionally believe in personal capital vis-a-vis psychic energy exchange. I use the world 'capital' poetically only."

"So then, is ur so-called 'poetic' concept of personal capital increased by ur celebrity status."

"My so called 'celebrity' status is marginal but remains something of a factor. All I'm saying is u misjudge the degrees to which…"

"The degrees to which what?"

"No that was it, just the degrees to which."

"The degrees to which ur celebrity status forces u into a role of responsibility u never explicitly asked for?"

"Now don't go putting words in my mouth."

"I think ur just making excuses for urself."

"Maybe I am, what are u doing?"

"I'm calling u out."

"I know but what are u actually doing."

"Do u consider urself a leader?"

"There is no leader, we all follow each other, look I'm on a date with my wife, can I call u back?"

"All good man, I've been recording this convo, think I have what I need here."

"Tight."

Not my best interview but fuck it, hopefully he got a lil pull quote for his story.

"Now where were we?"

"How come u got mad?"

"I wasn't mad."

"U sounded mad."

"I was just talking like slightly louder than normal."

"U sounded mad."

"I wasn't mad I was just excited."

"U sound mad right now."

"I'm not mad, I guess I was talking loud because I was a little excited and now I'm still talking kinda loud because I'm still riding in that leftover energy. Also I just talk loud, that's how I was raised."

"You sound aggressive."

"That's racist."

"Don't play that with me."

"I'll play whatever I want with whomever at whatever time."

"Why did u get excited?"

"He was trying to rattle me, prod a quote out of me."

"Why did u take the bait?"

"I had to give him something, it was an interview, sheesh quit busting my balls, no respect, a nigga can't win around here."

"Ay forget about it, take a walk, blow off some steam, meet u in Chapter 91."

I didn't really need to blow off any steam but I took a walk anyway, seemed like a good idea.

Along the way to Chapter 91 I got a lil lost.

I was trying to get to a "one day turned into the next" or "the ocean waves churned ceaselessly" and etc. but I just kept running into dead ends.

Hit up Chuy's for a Pacifico. He was out of Pacifico, I got an Indio. Went to go take a piss saw a staircase I had never seen before, narrow leading up to a thin door, walked up in and thru and to a room, plush, wallpapered, realized I was in a recording booth, kicked a dope verse:

PEACE ALLAH ZIG ZAG
UNIVERSAL
LEVEL SEVEN
TRANSPORTATIONAL
WINE SIPPER
YOUNG JACK LONDON
OR JOHN LENNON
WHATEVER
IM TRIPPIN
PEACE TO MITCH RICHMOND
MY POSSES ON BROADWAY
SEE ME IN A LONG CANDLE LIT HALLWAY

YOUNG FALL GUY
IM ALL HIGH AND WHATNOT
BUT IM HERE LIKE WHERE THE BUCK STOP
RIGHT NOW
ECSTATIC LABOR
EMBROILED KINETIC
YOUNG LITERATE
WORDS GO FIGURE EM
CLASSIC LIT
NO NIGGA JIM
OKONKWO
TUTUOLA
DOG IM A GOD IM A SOULJAH
HAPPY UMOJAH
METANOIA
RESHAPING THE WORLD
CHAOS AND CHANGE
TRAGICOMIC REALITY
BRAINWASHING IS A REAL AND DAILY
    OCCURRENCE
WE'RE ATTUNED TO MULTIPLE CURRENTS
HYPERSUBCONCIOUS TELEPATHIC
THERES A SCIENCE TO MAGIC
ITS ALL STONED SEMANTICS
UR BOY OUT HERE LAMPING
BRING THE FIRE LIKE CAMPING
CHAMPION
IM ONLY DANCING
SHOUT OUT TO LANSING MICHIGAN
SHOUT TO THE DETROIT LIONS
IM LISTENING TO COIT CRYING

WHO BRAVED THE COLD PLAINS OF THE
NORTH FOR THESE FOUL AND FORGET-
TABLE TECHNOLOGIES?
THE HARSH, FRIGID AIR IS REMEMBERED IN
THE BONES, THE VERY MARROW,
DOTH ANGELS DARE TO PART THEY LIPS
FOR A POOR DEVIL SUCH AS UR BOY? YAY
METHINKZ.
ALACK! GODS AND DEVILS ARE THE SAME
SPIRITUAL CREATURE DRAP'D IN
DIFF'RENT MASKS, OR MAYBE THE DEVIL
IS THE MASK AND THE GOD IS THE FACE,
OR MAYBE...

Oh there it is, Chapter 91.

91.

We met up in Chapter 91, at The Actual Cafe on San Pablo and I don't know, the late 20's maybe.

She was drinking a coffee, I was drinking a half Rosemary mint strawberry lemonade and half lavender Lapsang Souchong iced tea with a dash of my own añejo dulce from the flask.

We talked about whatever it was she wanted to talk about that day, maybe Shiraz, or the Internet, or the Sacred Order of this or that alien theology she was reading up on, or some penny stock money schemes.

I was soaking that up and shooting it back whenever need be-ed, buzzing along, zooming, zonin, only mildly zonked out.

I was feeling alphabetical, gubernatorial.

Felt like Vladimir Gutierrez, Yoenis Cespedes, et Cetera.

The Mambo Kings Were playing their songs of Love.

I felt like Kaizer Jose or whoever it was, that guy.

I felt like that guy, that dude.

She kept talking, at, thru, into, around me, she shaped me, she had a mesmerizing means of conversation, I enjoyed it.

The conversation was joyous, overjoyous sometimes, esctatic, laborious, at times, poetic even.

The conversation sheared off like 1 pound of water weight, made for some sheer muscle growth, the heart rate quickened and slowed, aerobic, I felt my core tighten.

We were trying to find an agreeable tempo.

Eventually we found it and it was off to the races.

"Truth is reality."

"What does that mean?"

"Earth, silence."

"The poem is broken, an unadvanced creature."

"The wilderness is-"

"IS WHAT?!"

"Well it isn't what it is so much as what it isn't-"

"And what isn't it then?"

"Well the question ain't so much what isn't it as what ain't it."

"Wait, who's who? Are you me or you, am I you or me?"

"Ur u, I'm me."

"And we are all together."

"Jah Rastafari."

"YEMAYA"
"CHANGO"
"YEMAYA"
"CHANGO"
"ALLAH MARIA YEMAYA"

And so on and so forth in that manner.

It was pleasantries and pleasances.

We occasionally wondered what we were doing there but put it out of mind, focused on just being there.

It was a lil cold but maybe more like pleasantly crisp mane iono.

Our styles were unorthodox.

Still are.

Man I feel like Stephen King man.

Bruh, I'm wearing a sweatshirt, I feel like Earl Sweatshirt.

Oh what I used that one already? Fuck it that's funny, I'ma say it twice, it's my book.

Shout out ya mama.

Haha mane, iono

Peace Amaze 88 bruh, I wrote a book how u like that?

Peace Loren Hell aka Saint John Denver the Last Dinosaur Junior Senior Executive CEO Speedwagon Wheels on the Busta RhymeSayers Entertainment Televisionary Dreamstate Representative Democracy Now Hear This Old Man He Played One Life to Live From New York It's Saturday Night Rider'Die Die My Darling Nikki Giovanni Martinelli Apple Cider I Hardly Knew Her Majesty's Theatre London Dungeons & Dragon's Breath of Fresh Heir to the Throne of Glass Eye Could Do This All Day…

Shout Fat Tony

Houston make some noise

Bruh, what else?

OK um… Man, what chapter is this? 91?

Cool so we on the countdown man, top ten (no particular order):

Water, SUNLITE
CHANGO, YEMAYA
Allah
Jah Rastafari
Huitzilopochtli
Ganesh 7 Kama
Allah Jah CHANGO
YEMAYA
Born
Cipher complete

So this is chapter born water SUNLITE aka born knowledge

It's simple mathematics.

92.

We were at the crib watching Half Baked when the electricity went out.

We lit some candles and drank beers on the deck.

Lights came back on we played records instead of watching TV.

Over the next stretch of hours, we played all the records in the box in a row:

- Mozart piano concertos no.s 12 &14
- ? And the mysterions
- Mingus ah um
- Selda
- High tide, green grass
- Ghetto music
- Sgt. pepper
- Augustus Pablo
- Songs of earth water fire and sky
- The Devils trill
- Buena vista social club
- Off the wall
- Billie holidays greatest
- It's monk's time
- Satie
- Music of North Africa
- a record that just said Middle East on it
- Monk and Trane at Carnegie hall
- Francoise Hardy
- Joaquin Rodrigo
- Antologia de la Musica Afro-Cubana
- The mops
- Miles ahead
- Getz/Gilberto
- Bitches brew
- Gounod's Faust
- Turkish Folk Dance Music
- Another Mozart record
- Santana abraxis
- Space is the place
- Last poets
- Ponca peyote songs

- Sly stone fresh
- Fate in a pleasant mood
- Free jazz
- Monastic trio
- Watermelon man
- Big bad beautiful day
- Mingus double antho
- Gregorian chants
- Criss cross
- Cosmic music
- Creedence Clearwater Revival
- Bunny wailer protest music
- Sun ship
- Tequila
- (Wes Montgomery)
- OUD
- egberto gismonti
- Vincentico Valdes y la Sonora maestra no wait Sonora Matancera
- Rolling Stones flowers
- Younger lovers
- Marvin Gaye
- Kinda blue
- Party animal
- Bloodstone natural high
- Ray Charles: Ray Charles
- Love supreme
- Blues and the abstract truth
- Africa unite
- Uprising
- Caetano veloso
- Islamic liturgy

- Leadbelly
- Mongo Santamaria drums and chants
- Pharaoh sanders
- Diamond life

And I don't know them all off top I think I'm missing a few, we were doing a lot of drinking at the time, mostly tequila.

It all started to sound like the same beautiful song.

By the time we got to the last record, sketches of Spain, Miles Davis, it was hot out.

We went down to the ocean and jumped in, found a skool o' Dolphins swam along side them asking them questions about their day.

"How was ur day?"

"Same old."

Swam on.

93.

Chapter 93 opens with a dog pissing on a lonely cactus at nite.

Off on out yonder a coyote skwooks its eerie howl, the stars twingle, the dog gets spooked and yaps into a slite gallup mid tinkle, finishes up, scampers off...

Maestro slid thru, children asleep, mama meditating. Marty and Malika over for dinner and just starting to crack beers.

I played dominoes w Maes' on the deck.

Offered him a beer.

"Oh, no thanks, I don't drink."

"I coulda swore… Eh, well, fuck it, more for me then."

He won the first game I won the next two then we both got bored on game four, switched to dice.

For no money tho, and different rules, any time u rolled a 7 u won, any time u rolled any other number u lost. I don't know what rules that is but we both won 6 and lost 6 a piece, tied.

As a tie breaker, we decided to hit the races, me, Maestro Allah, Marty. Lika and Dija caught up while Tima and Donna slept.

We went down to the track.

Marty bet 20 on Quickdraw Crockett and lost.

I bet 100 on California Chrome, won 350.

Maestron bet the 2 dollar exacta box payout and won 340.

We called it another tie but I felt he actually won that one, despite the numbers.

We lingered, drinking beers and whatnot, cut back to the crib.

Listened to all the records again.

They were all good records, a little academic sometimes as a collection but all very soulful and real.

Well, O.K.

94.

It was 5 in the morning. I was the only one up and I was drinking ice water watching the sunrise.

I felt 94 years old.

I felt like I was experiencing time as if I were a tree.

I was on two adderalls, two Norcos, some lean, a couple weed cookies some tequila, some beer, some mezcal and some red wine. I was feeling multilayered, my aura that of a psychic cake.

"For 3 days and 3 nites" I remember Mullah X telling me, "96 soldiers, that's born equality (we're all born equal) became trapped within the bosom of they very minds, the center of which is a point so infinitely vast as to be everything…"

He had went on in such a fashion, creating a mnemonic device, semantics withstanding, wired into the wetware of the human brain, triggerable at will, explaining with distinct certainty the extreme mathematical possibility of time travel. It took hours of explanation but I eventually understood what it was he was trying to convey and have been using that old chestnut ever since.

I smoked a cigarette, a pack of Marlboros materialized at some point.

The world seemed very boring, I may very well have fallen asleep in some sort of awkward waking position. Or at least been blacked out prob looking near comatose.

I was probably looking kinda ugly.

I had on some French reading glasses, I became aware of this and felt a percentage point uglier for this. My feelings of inferiority were most likely being generated by the French reading glasses, I'm pretty sure Frantz Fanon mentions this somewhere in Black Skin, White Masks…

Bruh truth be told, I felt like a house plant.

Bruh, I was hella high.

Felt like a skeleton.

A mosquito buzzed in my ear and brought me back to reality for a split second before I plunged into some other brand new internal madness, it was kind of fun in its own terrifying way.

Somehow managed to put on a record, Love Supreme, old fave. Real Classical Music.

I swam stationary thru the music.

Emotions, the ego, all things past, melted from my consciousness.

I forgave everybody including myself.

I begged the universal mother spirit for her ultimate forgiveness, she became me and we wept.

Word life reality peace god immaculate.

Everybody woke up at once. Marty and Malika went on a walk with Tima and Donna and so me and Dija just kicked it in bed.

Anne slid thru with her 3 cats, Napoleon, Zarathustra, and Lao Tze.

We sat around smoking opium and drinking tea.

Anne pontificated on hella topics, she used to mash with El Maestro Allah and they both can hold court.

Bruh.

She had some wild stories.

The opium felt nice.

All of a sudden it was pitch black nite with a brite wite muun.

Tima and Donna came flying thru, each standing on minor Rosegold falcons of their respective inventions. I was wowed to the floor. The couch, really, I mean to say, I laid down on the couch. Plucked Bobby D's pulp rag Tarantula off the coffee table flipped thru it: it was tite.

Took a lil nap.

Had a dream that I was hella good at basketball. It felt weird to be that good at basketball. It felt hella cool. Made me want to learn how to get hella good at playing basketball.

Had some other dreams too. U kno how that all go.

Anyway…

95.

It was the 95th chapter and things were starting to wind down. Somewhere along the way from there to here, we broke the 4th, 5th, 6th and 7th walls, and we now find ourselves here at this point, fully enlightened already and just counting down the last five chapters, only casually interested in what else might occur in this lil diegesis, curious as 2 why, now that we've transcended the physical world, we're still here holding this ream of bleached tree pulp, deciphering a series of three or so thousand year old symbols rendered in a liquified mineral stain. I guess the answer is we haven't, like we had first assumed, transcended the physical realm quite yet, so sadly, we have to keep going.

Anyway, I was giving a lecture at Yale School of Divinity. I had not prepared anything and I was pretty high but I felt in the zone enough:

"Hi kids. Sup y'all, how u doing. That's what's up. The homie James went here, studied Art History I think? Y'all know him? No? School of Divinity's a whole different thing huh? And plus he graduated hella long ago. Anyway, yea I was just trying to kill some time, I had not prepared any notes, full disclosure, my fault. Fina freeball this one.

"Anyway, the Divine is within, above below, at all sides, the Divine is most righteous and sublime, the Divine is most excellent, the Divine is syncretic, quantum, metanoic, et cetera.

Follow me, follow me, follow me, like snoop said, an old reggae refrain he picked up smokin treebo, what else? Oh yah, 2-Pac cares if ain't nobody else care, what else, come along with me to the butterflies and bees, we can wander thru the forest and do so as we please mane, I'm sure u all heard of this.

Only 25 people have ever left the earth's atmosphere, and they all are wild spiritual. U come to an epiphany in space. U ever been on a mountain or a big hill looking over a huge swath of land and sea? It's like that but insanely superior. Only 25 people on earth have ever felt that way, imagine their swagger, that swag is magnanimous, mayhaps even burdensome to the spiritually ill-prepared, true knowledge is a burden until it's unlocked and becomes the eternal gift of transcendence.

"Bruh, get acquainted with the natural world, the sun and sea, the trees mane. Nature, resplendent, kaleidoscopic, truth, beauty, the holy spirit mane it's all divine, Mashallah, Ave Maria, Allah Hu Akbar, Om Srim Hrim Lakshmi Biu

Namaha, Yemaya Yemaya, bless up bless up, L'Chaim, Jah Rastafari, etc.

"If u read up on the matter u'll find that I'm right. Language is a trick but it still points to a truth, word life reality peace God immaculate apocryphal the unfounded text beyond text, spirit hovering above flesh, ya trick, ya!

"Uh, what else… Binky binky boo binky binky. Rikkitikkitantikkitantantikkitikki. BUYAKA BUYAKA. Boom shakalaka Bing Bong wow.

"Forever is composed of nows. Every single moment is now. Now, now, now.

"NOW!"

Thunderous applause mane, I was a hit with these kids.

I hop a flying carpet back to the crib, kiss the wife and daughters, take a 12 hour nap, wake up tired, sleep another 12 hours, wake up again, finally refreshed.

Wife and daughters hit the beach, I didn't feel like it today, instead smoked weed and watched TV, logged onto Datpiff.com caught up on some recent mixtures, Curren$y, Migos, Soulja Boy, Stalley, Future, Young Thug, Whiz, Boat, everything seemed to be chugging along at the same rate.

Beat hella levels of Candy Crush on my phone, deleted Candy Crush, went down to the beach, kicked it with the wife and kids.

Fausto as always, was elsewhere. Nobody was worried about him, least of all him.

Ay bruh the days move into other days mane that's how time work mane.

96.

Trust nobody
The truth is out there
The truth is out here
No filibustering
Defibrillate

That's the new five commandments, remember those.
Matterfact here's the next 5:
Never have a broken hot tub
Bless up bless up
Jah Rastafari
CHANGO
YEMAYA

Ay but CHANGO
ALLAH JAH RASTAFARI CHANGO YEMAYA
HUIZOPOTCHTLI
CHIPOTLE
CHIPOTL
Wait another 5 is
6 no broke hot tubs
7 is foreplay & penetración
8, it is ur party
9 grow
10 party

We were at some hotel in LA called the Ataya or Abaya or naw wait it was the Arayan (unfortunately appropriated ancient name), a Persian intellectual cafe hotel, and we were stoned at the swimming pool thinking up lists of various commandments, we were in a happy state of growth.

Anyway my wife had stolen a keycard to the penthouse suite, and we wandered our way over there, I felt like the black Steve King.

Felt high off myself.

Wandered along, led by beauties.

Rosemary, incense, candles

The truth eternal, shelter, sanctuary

Emoji font, Happy Heiro Day, the codified def, Perpetual art life, life Art perpetua, wherefore art life, perpetua, Word preserveth, et cetera

Hard knowledge, terrors, wonders, overs, unders

Most heardabout, intelligent

Black man

Original

This is Allah, Jah, CHANGO

yo it's the real

We was off arag I think it was called who knos

Anyway where was I, yeah we did our thing man we drank some wine then some whiskey

Smoked a joint or 2 maybe 3 I don't remember

Was feeling magnificent like Gandhi

Wasn't sure if, wait what?

Somebody mentioned the concept of evil, the room worked to rid evil of its consciousness to mixed results

Language itself desensitizes the mind from itself.

Now.

Now remains.

The soul grows a skin

Truth becomes reality

Deafens, blinds, makes weak, rends time, rips ferocious, shreds the gnar, jams, makes, breaks, takes, scrapes, occasionally this that, peace Allah CHANGO

Inner dialogue compared to centrifugal force that's synergy dog.

Lyrical, annotated.

Feel like dfw, nirvana dude, kirko bangz, etc

Writing important things, I truly do believe that

This is dumb.

Naw whatever this is OK.

97.

The note taker

The water tester

Taster

The fire blazer

Trailblazer peace to Portland

Oregon

Lames play aimless

Dangereauex et setera

Bruh it was the 97th chapter of my 100 chapter novel, yeah the chapters got short sometimes, yea the more I smoke the smaller the Philly get yeah et setera

Yes I'm counting the chapters down, these are victory laps

If u do it right

All laps are victory laps if u do it right
Truth peace glory
Trill immaculate
Abundant
Privileged styles like young Nosferatu
The you me alluvus

Hey u kno what I was at a bar in a mall in LBC listening to a live Jimi Hendrix cover and I wasn't mad.

I tipped the bartender 777 dollars, left, pissed on a beautiful palm tree.

Imagine a world where every literary detail made huge political difference in the collective narrative. Some major pro poets live like that, so just remember that sad, happy, beautiful, ugly and interesting fact.

To write a major work in the English that's tight PERO pa hacerlo en e'pañol e' un'otra cosa

Not to mention all the other lenguajes…

Man this book is tight I don't care what nobody say this shit hella real.

Hey don't look at me, watch TV, don't shoot the messenger that's just how it came thru ur boy.

Existence is prismatic, exclamatory.

When u get caught between the moon and New York City (I know it's crazy but it's true) the best that u can do is fall in love.

We were on the freeway in Southern California at nite listening to the radio in stunned disbelief at the audacity of the machine.

We flipped to some rock en español like what? Ayyy!

Existence is truth, bless up.

What a book, soak up these knowledges.

Zim zimma who got the keys to the beema, furl meh.

Shake Shake Shake. Shake Shake Shake. Shake ur booty. Shake ur booty.

Etc.

Truth immaculate.

Try to understand, try to understand, try try try to understand: I'm a magic man.

Like, Wow, Man.

Truth, Behold.

Y'all So Stupid.

Truth, magnificent.

We kept flipping channels til we found what we needed: pure poetry, linguistic freedom.

At this point we folded in on ourselves like beautiful umbrellas.

Who knows or cares, am I rite?

What's today's math, Born God? Or…

Whatever, who cares. Today is the shadow of yesterday. What's the shadow of yesterday's math? Trick question, yesterday's math is today's literary truth. Bless up. Swag infinitum.

Allah Jah CHANGO.

98.

I was wearing a T shirt.

Sitting on a bed.

Next to my wife:

She was in meditation and me too, actually.

I felt like Toni Morrison but cis male

I'm a Scorpio

So u kno

Cualquier cosa or whatever

We had written ourselves into a little shrubbery maze, those occur, some people even live in them, some say u can never escape them.

We tuned into Dona y Tima's Perfect Beautiful Everything and carved a little caveman opera out for ourselves to watch, the light rendering it vividly upon our consciousnesses.

We meditated for real, I'm not even joking about that part.

Movement.

Swag swag Jah CHANGO Allah chango

I sneezed twice, a rare occurrence, almost felt like a joke, I had pretty much eliminated all illness when I converted to Islam.

I took a drink of water. Said a Hail Mary.

Let's hit the beach, wifey said "I kno the 1".

Ma' norte, surferos

Marty and Malika were there with the homie Moose Moose, his girl Faith and Faith mama Estelle was there cookin bwoy, pinay food, lumpia, that clear noodle joint what they call that one again that go hard, what else, oh yea we was drinking, u kno, playing a lil pusoy dos, small chips, 500 peso buy in, they were like "come surfing with us in the morning, I went surfing, I was bad at it but it was tight regardless, I surfed on down to paradise city where the girls are pretty or however that song go ay bruh iono mane ur boy just here filibustering

Linguistic reality has a cartoon quality

The icon, the font, the roaring buzz saw beak bird the sleeping waters the pixelated specters in hallowed chambers

Faith transports reality across its own spacetime

Confusion is a moment within the atom.

The mask scars the face.

Are glasses real? What do they do, do they work?

Society flexes upon itself.

The sacred geometry of the universe is very swag.

Swag, eternal, immaculate.

I'm high in this bitch.

Feel like Kirko Bangz, feel like Nassim Haramein.

Money is a sickness, but vision a vaccine.

Fear is a weapon, love is a tool.

Strength, speed.

The forces of nature.

Sleep, pleasure, flowers.

Believe these patterns.

Game, eternal

Swag infinity

Bars, truth, wonder.

Citadels, oceanic lite

The process

Los Angeles

San Francisco

Dungeonous, wavy

Fun genius, myth, labor...

There is absolutely no difference between anything

Aim for sustainable joy

The video game

The visual war game

The art projects, the projects

Truth, vanishing, reappearing, change, flux, chaos, order, understanding....

Lyrical mountains

Swag Allah

Poetry, commerce, leaves, offers, recreational motorists, presuppositions, cafe correcto, people really be searching for freedom and meaning, happiness, please understand the extra linguistic necessity of beautiful love, love beautiful.

Labyrinth ideal accessoried by lite

Yin yang Allah

Yo soy un monstro

Bars unequivocal

Truth, tru truth

Pan global, humanity, intuition

U demand consistency

U demand

Why?

I demand magnanimous truth

Peace, real

Love

Truth

Beauty

The super God cosmic spiritually pure and whatnot la pura viva la raza mama Africa AYAYAY marijuana y Paz a la isla

Historic images rendered by modern machine

The infinite now

Karaoke, beautiful

Petite swan, peyote karaoke, coyote hillz, the moon waters

Peace Allah Sorry House

I truly am sorry, def, whispering in a cold kwiet nite, love life laff joy kinetic

Overheard: "everything makes sense"

High in a living room watching TV, occasional debate, much filibustry…

Swag apartmental accoutrements

Music video channels, Windows, late capitalist tea parties, Eagle rental, cacti, motorcycles, feelings, viva la resistancia, the perpetual LSD choking game across global chess boards, the advanced theater troupes of congress, the watchdogs, the synagogue minstrels, the cantorial horsebetters, yay, the ay man ay dog ay, the literal silhouettes, sunken vessels, sunchild MOONCHILD soul rebelmatic soy un monstro party animal party animal peaceful solutions OK, Word word ok ok no doubt thaswasup CHANGO

Race, ciphers, the circular patterns, poem, real life, water, juice.

Bless up bless up.

Anyway that was 98, Born Build/Destroy peace Allah see u in Born Born or whatever

99.

I had taken some acid the nite before and was still a little bit on the acid, it was early afternoon, ambling around LA in a Honda Accord super incognegro, listening to a Ruben Gonzalez CD, Muslim bride by my side, bbz with Medina, we went scooped them, got stoned with Medina, she was listening to Kodak Black, good trap music, I was fucking w it.

Decided to drive up to the yay break bread with some O.G.s plus I had a package to scoop in ghost town and some fools in the rich owed the kid some yaper.

The one was beautiful but too slow, the 5 was quicker but less beautiful and still slow, we hopped on the 777, a new freeway Tima and Dona had manifested with their Beautiful Perfect Everything. It was fast and beautiful, as we were.

Oh wait it wasn't a Honda Accord it was a matte black 2016 Camaro. Also fast and beautiful. Wifey commented it was kind of a white people car, Tima and Dona recalibrated their Beautiful Perfect Everything.

It wasn't a matte black 2016 Camaro, it was a red Ferrari La Ferrari. Italian. Who don't like Italians?

"Once u invent ur own reality, can it be uninvented?" Tima asked.

"It was already there, u just opened ur consciousness to it."

"O.K." Don(n)a said.

We were quiet for a second, I put on Kokomo Arnold.

Dona: "Invention doesn't exist?"

Yo: "Sure it does, its nature is illusory, it sits just outside its semantics."

Tima: "Poetics are the math of the intuition?"

Yo: "Sure, yeah, now y'all getting it."

Dija put her two cents in:

"Now is the time to know, everything we do is sacred."

"Peace Allah."

"No doubt."

We sped along the triple sev, thru the breathing conduits of the Beautiful Everything.

"Nothing is perfect," said Tima.

"So is everything," said Donna.

We saw an exit for Troubadorial Heights, missed it, took the next one, Cherry Tree Hill, gassed the tank, had a champagne at the local Italian restaurant, forgot the name.

We drove on.

A cop pulled us over, I shot him with a Sterling Silver Six Shooter, like BANG yer dead copper.

We ditched the Ferrari La Ferrari, hopped a flying carpet, ended up in Shiraz, hopped a yellow gold falcon, ended up in The Pain, hopped a rose gold hawk ended up on Planet X, hopped the white gold eagle ended up in some Cartesian embroidery, hopped the embroidery itself, ended up in u. Why did u open this book and read it up to this page? U tell me. Cause I don't know.

Why did I write it up to this page? I had made a deal, I figured it would make me a little more money to live on but also because I enjoyed it, it was something to do.

What does it all mean? I don't know.

But I do think it's a damn fine book or at the very least pretty O.K. Or matter fact u kno what it's hella good. Bruh, this book is amazing. Son, this book is flames. Fuego.

We kept driving, I looked out the window up at the brite blu sky. The sun's brilliant fuego.

The Beautiful Perfect Everything.

The moon, it was nite now, the stars, the slightly frigid air, wait now it was warm, a nice gust of desert wind, no wait the heat was hot but there was a slight water to it, what do u call that? Tropical.

We were on a beach now, soft sand, mellow waves. I felt like Fidel Castro, I felt like A Tribe Called Quest, all of them, felt like a half white KRS ONE, felt like the Chinese 2Pac, felt like the Mexican Chris Rock.

We all have pretensions, like pre-tensions, like previous tensions, but when we refuse to differentiate the past from the present, we deny the possibility of numerous worthwhile futures.

Truth, eternal, peace, infinity.

We found ourselves galloping on horses.

Thru citrus orchards.

The beautiful unhinged reality of it left us bereft, stilted, an aluminumesque lean-to.

I considered robotics as a concept, then moved onto matters more spiritual.

The end is endless bars, nonstop bars of sand sectoring seas between shallows and deeps, the end is an endless globe of sea, speckled with islands.

Somewhere along the way, I got trained to go, and I can't seem to untrain myself.

A wall is a concept, it can be paper thin.

We can dislodge the terror from the boulders of our hearts.

This is truly (a) novel.

(B) a novel

© or what

Feel like Vic Mensa mane

I'm composing riddles for mass consumption from my solid gold chariot, Young Privilege.

True poetry refuses, insists, reminds u of its names

I used to sell dope of all kinds but not anymore.

What is The Literal?

I've been in congress with moon children and sun children alike, in all manners of twilight, I'm a child of electrum, please don't let me be misunderstood. Art is self-espionage, extra-computational, post algorithmic, why do birds sing, etc.

Empirical authenticity, pseudo linguistic, flight…

Ecstatic knowledge can terrify momentarily, but that is only a skin of fear shedding away.

Narrative persists, I lit a cigarette in the past and took a drag, looking at my surroundings. The past looked just like the present and the future didn't look like anything, it was unknowable.

I took a sip of water, meditated, got a beer, drank that, I took a long walk, ended up at an airport, flew to Italy, got in a fight with a Airport Security Guard, he probably won on points, the fascists go off points a lot over there, but I got some nice solid duffs in.

I flew to the UK they put me in jail for a day I beat this Persian dude at chess. Where did the chess board come from? I didn't ask/care. In retrospect, I wonder tho.

Flew to Switzerland (couldn't tell u where), stayed in a very nice hotel out there, I took a walk to a park and beat a Frenchman at chess, bruh I was on a roll, I flew to Barcelona and recited Lorca in some Absynth Bar that Picasso supposedly kicked it at at some point, got fucked up on Absynth, but had to catch a flight back to the Beautiful Perfect Everything, from where apparently I had never left.

I felt like Ernest Hem-dog in Moveable Fiesta but only slightly wavier.

I smoked weed out of a bong the homie Mira had fashioned out of an old copy of Infinite Jest. Spencer was there too. I felt like the black Tao Lin.

I felt like Mos Def 007, like Jimi 3000, like Oakland Tech 9, etc.

We stopped by an old river and drank from its waters, it was clean.

We felt miraculous, unpunctuated, unadorned by pretense, backs unbent under weightless reference, free mane.

The minor scale is anything but. Its pivot is in its halfstep.

Music, what a miraculous lil waste of time. Only thing worth doing probably.

We ended up in Reykjavik, listening to Erykah Badu. I flipped thru a copy of Black Elk Speaks.

Tima said: "looks nice out here."

Donna: "Regal, poetical."

Dija said: "We should buy a home out here."

I said: "no doubt, no doubt."

100.

"Bye bye."

We mobbed up into The Beautiful Perfect Everythang and sailed away.

We didn't leave the world so much as transform it into our own.

We melded into the supersoul and rested upon the cosmic cushion of love.

U were there.

Ur there right now.

Ur here right now to be exact but semantics are useless out here in the Beautiful Perfect Everything, it's no language here.

These aren't even words ur seeing or hearing or thinking, they're the echoes of a memory of a feeling, and the feeling ur feeling right now is now.

U are u now, always were, always will be.

It was always now. It is. It will be.

Now is the only time, the realest/realist time, the time is now.

The meme and reference shed like snakeskin and fall the cosmic corners of the dusty chambers of ur consciousness, we are blasted clean by the infinitely magnanimous lite rayz of existenz.

We the bold journeyers parade on, emboldening exponentially, the boldest snow boulder, the universal pearl, here we are.

Goodbye and hello, there's no end, there was no beginning, goodbye is hello. We have ascended, expanded, the illusory hallucination of reality quivers, shatters, allows us to escape, but to where? To reality, of course.

Bruh, what don't u understand?

Ur free, u can go now! U can put this book down and live ur life mane.

In The Perfect Beautiful Everything the word bruh exists as a gender neutral title, in PBE it's no language, in the PBE it's a big beautiful time bruh bruh

I copped some J's, a new A's fitted and a bag of H.

We hit the beach, sunny resort beach. I surfed for the next 77 hours.

It's good for the heart, surfing.

Surfed on down Mexico way, stopped there gazed at the ocean, beautiful ceaseless waves.

Jah Rastafari Allah Jah CHANGO YEMAYA furl meh?

DO. YOU. FEEL ME?

Regardless of whether or not u feel me, here I am and here u are. Have a good one.

Much love.

O.K?